CHRISTMAS DANGER

HAZARDOUS HOLIDAY

LYNN SHANNON

CHRISTMAS DANGER

Copyright © 2021 by Lynn Balabanos

Published by Creative Thoughts, LLC

All rights reserved.

No part of this book may be reproduced in any form or by any electronic or mechanical means, including information storage and retrieval systems, without written permission from the author, except for the use of brief quotations in a book review.

This book is a work of fiction. Names, characters, businesses, organizations, places, events and incidents either are the product of the author's imagination or are used factitiously. Any resemblance to actual persons, living or dead, events, or locales is entirely coincidental.

Cover design by Maria Spada.

Scripture appearing in this novel in whole or in part from THE HOLY BIBLE, NEW INTERNATIONAL VERSION®, NIV® Copyright © 1973, 1978, 1984, 2011 by Biblica, Inc.™ Used by permission. All rights reserved worldwide.

May the God of hope fill you with all joy and peace as you trust in him, so that you may overflow with hope by the power of the Holy Spirit.

Romans 15:13

ONE

A scrape echoed behind her.

Holly Miller glanced over her shoulder. Darkness, broken only by the occasional streetlight, stretched down the block. Was someone there? Or had she imagined the sound?

She peered into the shadows. Something shifted.

Holly's breath quickened. She clutched her car keys tighter, and the metal cut into the soft flesh of her palm. An icy wind blew a paper napkin across the empty church parking lot. Everyone else had gone home over half an hour ago. Holly had stayed late to clean the church's recreational room.

She was alone. In a dark parking lot.

The sensation of being watched crept over her. The same feeling had plagued her for the last few weeks. In the grocery store. At church. While taking a run in the neighborhood. Yet every time she turned to look, no one was there.

Holly waited one heartbeat. Then another.

A cat raced from the darkness. It streaked past the main entrance and skirted around the back of the building.

Holly released the breath she was holding as relief weakened her knees. She chuckled. Her imagination was running away with itself, a side effect of living for so long in Boston. No one was lurking in the shadows to attack her. Not in Cutler, Texas. The tiny town was tucked two hours away from Austin. It wasn't crime free—Holly knew that from her job as a social worker—but serious incidents were extremely rare.

She forced her muscles to relax by taking another deep breath. The air fogged in front of her. Christmas was next week. They wouldn't have snow, but it would be cold. Holly picked up her pace. Down the street, Christmas lights were strung on the shops, and a wreath decorated the bakery door. The scent of gingerbread lingered in the crisp air. It soothed her jittery nerves and the last of her anxiety melted away.

She loved Christmas. Everything about it spoke to her heart.

"Silent night, holy night…" Holly sang the familiar tune, her voice carrying through the night. The church choir was performing at the Cutler Christmas Festival in a few days. Holly was the event coordinator, and while it was a lot of work, every bit of effort was worth it. The money raised aided families in need within their community. It paid for elderly residents' yard work, bought groceries for those unexpectedly unemployed, and helped families with hospitalized children.

She rounded the corner into an alley between the church and adjacent stores. Her sedan sat like a hunched giant halfway down. The parking lot had been full when Holly arrived late to choir practice. She'd been lucky to find a spot in the alley.

The light on the side of the church was out. She hadn't noticed that before but made a mental note to mention it to Pastor Sam.

Her footsteps echoed against the asphalt. Darkness wrapped around her like a cloak. Another gust of wind rippled through her hair, causing a curl to get caught on her lip gloss. Holly swiped at the wayward strand before hitting the button on her fob. Her sedan beeped, the headlights flashing for a brief moment.

Long enough to catch the man-sized shadow arcing toward her.

The attacker slammed into her with the force of a freight train. Holly collided with the wall of the church, car keys tumbling from her fingers as pain blinded her. Air whooshed from her lungs.

The man pressed against her. She was trapped between him and the wall, unable to move. Inside her head, she was screaming, but her lungs were starved of oxygen. Nothing more than a weak wheezing escaped her lips. The rough brick scraped her cheek.

What did he want? Her wallet? Her car? He could have them both. Holly sucked in a pitiful breath.

"Take it." Her purse, knocked off her shoulder in the initial assault, dangled from her elbow. "I'll give it to you. There's no need to hurt me."

The attacker ignored her. Had he even heard Holly's whispered plea? Fear, thick and soupy, sludged through her veins. Her curly hair, flung free of her winter cap, blocked her vision. Holly tried to suck in another breath, but her lungs wouldn't expand due to the pressure against her back. Dots danced across her vision.

Suddenly, he backed off. Holly pulled in a desperate, shallow breath.

Rough hands gripped her biceps, and the assailant dragged her backward, deeper into the alley. Holly screamed. It came out weak, a side effect of not having a chance to catch her breath. She fumbled to get her feet underneath her, struggling to keep up with his rapid pace while moving in reverse. The alley had two access points. One ahead of them, and one behind. With a horrifying jolt, Holly realized this wasn't about her car or money. It wasn't a robbery.

The man wanted her. And he was dragging her to the opposite side of the alley where a potential getaway vehicle was waiting.

No, Lord. Please.

She couldn't go anywhere with him. Every self-defense instructor she'd ever had said it was harder to escape from a second location.

She had to stand her ground here. She had to fight harder.

Holly let her body go limp, catching the attacker off guard. He released her as they both tumbled into a puddle. Cold from the damp ground seeped into Holly's jeans. She barely registered it. Her heart jackhammered against her breastbone as she pushed to her hands and knees. She sucked in another deep breath and screamed again.

This time the blessed sound carried. But would anyone hear her? The street had been empty earlier, and given the late hour, chances were slim she'd be rescued by a bystander.

The attacker grabbed for her. Holly flung an elbow at his face and missed, hitting his neck instead. He grunted, rearing back with a curse. Holly didn't wait. She lashed out with her foot. It landed some place soft. The attacker yelped and tumbled back to the ground.

Holly scrambled to her feet. Another scream boiled inside her, but she couldn't dislodge it from her throat. Every instinct was focused on one thing.

Running. Getting away.

Survival.

Holly bolted. Her shoes pounded against the pavement and her breath came in puffs. Was he behind her? Chasing her? Her hair blocked her vision. Holly didn't dare waste a second to push it out of her eyes, nor did she glance behind her.

She could feel him. Coming for her.

The alley felt impossibly long. Like miles in her panicked state, instead of yards. She pumped more energy into her legs, narrowing her focus to the beckoning streetlights visible through the strands of her hair.

She burst out of the alley and into the street.

White headlights blinded Holly. She half-spun. An SUV barreled toward her, the screech of tires on the road shattering the night air.

TWO

Police Chief Aiden James jerked the steering wheel on his SUV, even as he slammed the brake pedal to the floor. The seat belt yanked on his shoulder. Aiden sent up a winged prayer as he barreled closer to the startled woman in the road. He caught a glimpse of a pale face and wide terror-filled eyes.

His front bumper slipped past the woman. Aiden had missed her.

Barely.

The SUV careened into the opposite lane and screeched to a halt. One of the rear tires rested on the sidewalk.

Aiden sucked in a breath. He peeled his fingers from the steering wheel and unhooked his seat belt. He could've killed the woman. A strong dose of anger heated his blood. Aiden jettisoned from the vehicle. "What on earth are you doing?"

The woman didn't move. Her back was to him, and she stood frozen in the center of the road. Aiden's steps faltered.

He'd know that red jacket and gorgeous mane of hair anywhere.

Holly Miller. She'd moved to Cutler six months ago. As a social worker, her job often intersected with Aiden's. They'd formed an easy friendship, one he was half tempted to make more. Until he remembered being left at the altar by his fiancée.

Once bitten, twice shy. Or something like that.

Why had Holly jumped in front of his patrol car? Aiden scanned the immediate area. The church was shut up tight and the street was quiet. Nothing seemed amiss, yet his hand dropped to the weapon at his hip. Holly was neither foolish nor reckless. If she'd run out in front of his vehicle, there'd been a reason.

"Holly?" He approached her from the side. "Are you okay?"

She didn't answer. Holly stared blankly down the road. Violent quakes shook her petite form. Her jeans were spattered with water and mud, as was the front of her coat. A scrape marred the curve of her cheek. Concern knotted in Aiden's stomach. She was in shock. What—or who—had done this to her?

Aiden's jaw tightened as emotions wrangled inside him. He longed to pull Holly into his arms, to comfort her and say everything was okay now. But that would be unprofessional and unwise.

His job was to protect her, and that's what he would do.

Aiden circled to stand in front of her and bent down until they were face-to-face. "Holly, it's me. Aiden. What happened?"

She blinked, as if being brought out of a dream. Aiden

saw the moment she recognized him. Stark terror replaced the blank expression on her face. Impossibly, the shakes racking her body intensified. She reached for him.

Aiden gave in to his desire to touch her by gently taking hold of her forearm. "What is it?"

Holly sucked in a breath. "S-s-someone a-a-attacked me...."

"Where?"

She lifted a slender hand and pointed. "There."

His gaze shot to the alley. It was shadowed. Was her attacker still lingering? Aiden immediately shifted into a protective posture. "Who was it?"

"I-I don't know."

"Come on." Keeping hold of Holly, he steered her to his vehicle. Aiden opened the passenger-side door and helped her inside. He quickly covered Holly with an emergency blanket. Shock could kill a person. His first priority had to be her.

Using the portable radio, Aiden called for backup. The police department was on the other side of town—a short two-minute drive away—but the other officers assigned to work were already on patrol. Dispatch gave him an ETA of four minutes.

"I don't want an ambulance." Holly interjected before Aiden could request one, along with the backup. "I'm okay."

He didn't agree. Her teeth were still chattering. "You're in shock."

"No, I'm fine. He...he just scared me." She swallowed hard. "Aiden, I don't think it was a robbery. The attacker didn't attempt to take my purse or my car. He grabbed me and started dragging me down the alley."

That knot in Aiden's stomach tightened. "Toward the other entrance?"

"Yes."

Holly could be wrong. Perpetrators didn't always act reasonably in the height of the moment since adrenaline often clouded a person's thoughts. Yet the sensation of being watched lingered, even now. As if someone was hiding in the shadows. It made Aiden's skin crawl and lent credence to Holly's assertion that this was more than a simple robbery gone sideways.

He assessed her. Holly's trembles were slowing. She met his gaze and her pupils seemed normal. Aiden made a split-second decision. "Keep the doors locked. Wait here for me."

He needed to check out the alley. If the attacker was still around, there was a possibility they could catch him tonight and end this.

"Where are you going?" Holly stopped him from shutting the door. "Wait, Aiden..."

Fear and worry creased the bow of her lips into a thin line. Somehow Aiden instinctively understood she wasn't worried about being left alone. No, she was scared he would get hurt. That was Holly. She fretted over everyone else. It was one of the things he'd noticed about her right away. She was selfless.

Which only increased Aiden's anger about the attack on her. He'd be upset over any assault in his town, but this? Hurting Holly infuriated him.

"Be careful," she said, reinforcing Aiden's suspicion about her concern.

"I'll be okay, Holly." He snapped the locks shut before

grasping the door handle. "Lay on the horn if you need to get my attention."

She nodded. Color had returned to her cheeks, painting them with a pretty pink blush, and her chin held a determined tilt. The shock was clearly fading.

Aiden shut the car door and used the portable radio to provide an update to the responding unit. They needed to proceed with caution.

A cold wind whistled down the street. Aiden pulled his service weapon but pointed it downward as he crossed to the alley. His heart picked up speed, but he consciously kept his breathing even. He removed a flashlight from his duty belt and clicked it on.

Using the wall of the church as cover, he peeked around the corner. Holly's car sat a short distance away. Shadows stretched toward the rear of the alley. Aiden couldn't see anyone, but he sensed someone was there.

"Police department! Come out with your hands up!"

A shadow shifted as the assailant ran down the alley. Judging from the height and bulk, it was a man. He was wearing dark clothes and a ski mask.

"Police!" Aiden shouted and raised his weapon. "Freeze!"

The man paid him no heed. He ducked into the darkness beyond the flashlight's beam.

Aiden gave chase, slowing as he reached the other end of the alley. It was foolish to race out blindly. The attacker could ambush him. Instead, Aiden again peeked around the corner.

The rev of an engine caught his attention. A dark-colored truck raced away from the curb. Mud spattered the license plate. Aiden shouted for the man to stop, but it was fruitless. The truck's taillights faded into the night.

Aiden hit the brick wall with the heel of his hand before updating his backup. Maybe the responding unit would catch the truck. It was a long shot, but it was something.

Using the flashlight, Aiden swept the alley. Holly's untouched purse sat in the center of a puddle and her car keys lay against the church wall. Her car doors were shut. Everything in the vehicle appeared undisturbed.

Aiden's grip tightened on the flashlight. The attacker had been in the alley for minutes after Holly escaped, yet he hadn't stolen her car or money.

Holly was right. Whoever this perpetrator was, he was after one thing.

Her.

THREE

The police department break room smelled like burnt coffee and stale pizza. Holly shifted in the hard-plastic chair. It'd been half an hour since the attack, and although her body had stopped trembling, the knot in the pit of her stomach hadn't abated. Why would anyone want to hurt her?

Holly didn't have a clue.

She'd given an initial statement to Aiden, and then an officer had driven her to the station to wait while the crime scene was processed. Holly would've preferred to go home, but leaving without her purse and car didn't seem prudent. Besides, she wanted to know what Aiden uncovered.

"Any dizziness?" Kasey Jacobs asked, a concerned furrow between her brows. The paramedic's patch on her shoulder was frayed and worn. "Or nausea?"

"Nope." Holly gave her friend a tight smile. "I'm fine. There was no need to call you."

"Aiden called me because some maniac assaulted you. He wants to make sure you don't need to go to the hospital."

Kasey turned to rummage in her bag. She pulled out gauze and antibiotic ointment. "Did you get a look at the attacker?"

Holly sighed. "No. It was dark and he was wearing a ski mask."

Kasey winced but didn't ask any other questions about the attack. Something Holly was grateful for. It'd been bad enough discussing it with Aiden, and her emotions were still tender. She was fighting back tears even now.

Kasey gently dabbed at Holly's cheek with the gauze. "This doesn't look bad. Any other scrapes?"

"I don't think so. My jacket took the worst of it."

"Thank goodness." Kasey's mouth pursed. Her long dark hair was pulled back into a ponytail, accenting her angular face. She glanced at Holly's cell phone on the table. The screen was cracked, but it had survived the attack. "Did you call your grandparents yet?"

"Yes. I debated putting it off, but the rumor mill in town runs fast. I didn't want Gram and Pop to hear about it from someone else first and panic."

Kasey nodded. "Smart decision. Officer Jacks is the biggest gossip. By morning, the entire town will know what happened."

"That's what I figured. Pop and Gram wanted to come home from their vacation immediately, but I insisted it wasn't necessary."

Her grandparents were on a trip to celebrate their fiftieth wedding anniversary. They were due back before Christmas. Holly hated calling them with the news of her attack since it would cause them to worry, but there was no alternative. Still, their whole trip didn't have to be ruined.

Her grandparents deserved to celebrate their wonderful marriage together.

"Okay, all done." Kasey tossed the gauze in the trash and flashed a smile. "Now your cheek won't fall off from infection." Her expression grew serious. "All joking aside, are you okay, Holly? Tonight was..."

"Scary. But yes, I'm okay. I'd just like to know who the attacker is."

"So would I," came a familiar voice.

Aiden. Holly's treacherous heart skipped a beat as he stepped over the threshold and into the break room.

The police uniform strained over his broad shoulders. His jaw was shadowed by late-night whiskers that highlighted the chiseled shape of his face. Aiden's mouth was drawn tight and his deep blue eyes were shadowed with concern. In one strong hand, he carried her purse.

Kasey slung the medic's bag over her shoulder. "I'm going to take off now. Holly, if you need anything, call me."

"Thanks, Kasey."

Her friend slipped from the room. Aiden set Holly's purse on the table. "I know it's late, but I have follow-up questions to ask. Is that okay?"

She nodded. Their gazes met and heat rose in Holly's cheeks. No matter how much she tried, this annoying attraction to the handsome lawman wouldn't go away. In fact, the more she got to know Aiden, the worse it became. He was smart and hardworking. Disciplined. Big-hearted. In many ways, Aiden reminded Holly of her beloved grandfather.

But becoming more than friends was impossible. Her parents' divorce had taught Holly that love always came at a cost. Cutler was her fresh start. A chance to lay down roots in a place where she belonged. Holly had no intention of messing things up by getting involved with the town's police chief.

Aiden pulled out the chair across from her and sat. "I know your attacker was wearing a ski mask, but did you recognize him at all? Maybe something he said sounded familiar?"

"No. I don't think he even spoke to me, and nothing about him was familiar." Holly hugged her arms around her midsection. "Was he still in the alley when you went to check?"

"Yes. I don't want to scare you, Holly, but I think your instincts are right. This doesn't follow the pattern of a robbery or a carjacking. Can you think of any reason why someone might want to hurt you?"

"No, but..." She swallowed hard. "Lately, I've had the feeling someone is watching me."

He frowned. "For how long?"

"The last few weeks."

Aiden leaned forward. "Why didn't you say anything to me?"

"Because I thought it was my imagination. Every time I got the feeling, I'd look and no one was there. I mean..." She bit her lip. "What was I going to say, Aiden? I would've sounded paranoid."

Except she hadn't been imagining it. Someone had been watching her. Waiting. Planning.

Stalking.

A shudder racked her body. Holly rose from her chair. She paced the length of the room, stopping at the glass wall separating the break room from the rest of the police station.

Her gaze bounced around. "You don't have any Christmas decorations up. Maybe you should get a tree for the entire station. A live one would make the place smell like Christmas, and it's no trouble to take care of as long as someone waters it every day—"

"Holly."

He said her name gently, the timbre of his voice undoing her resolve to be strong. Tears sprang to her eyes. She was rambling. It was easier to worry about Christmas decorations for the police station than the attack.

Holly swiped at the tears as they crossed her cheeks. "I'm sorry."

Aiden came to stand in front of her. "You have no reason to be sorry."

"I ran in front of your SUV. I nearly caused you to crash."

His mouth curled at the corners. "You'll do anything to get my attention."

She laughed in spite of herself before whacking him gently on the shoulder. "Cut it out, Aiden. You've got enough female admirers in this town. I won't join the club."

He chuckled, and then his expression grew serious. "We'll get to the bottom of this, Holly. I promise." He placed a reassuring hand on her shoulder. "Everything is going to be okay."

His touch soothed her raw emotions, and his confidence bolstered her own. Aiden was one of the most dedicated law enforcement officers she'd ever met. There was no one else she'd rather have watching her back.

Holly cleared her throat and wiped the last of the tears from her face. "Thank you, Aiden."

His blue eyes warmed. "No thanks necessary. You're the best social worker this town has ever had. I never thought Marcy Beckman would stop calling us out to her house three times a day."

Marcy was nearing seventy and lived on the edge of town. She called the police station so an officer would have to visit her. Marcy would ply them with sweet tea and conversation.

Holly chuckled. "Mrs. Beckman just needed company. She's very happy volunteering at the animal shelter."

"So I hear. Smart of you to have one of the employees pick her up on their way to work."

She shrugged. "It was an easy fix."

Aiden frowned, and his brow furrowed. "Holly, Mrs. Beckman isn't the only one you've helped. Remember the run-in you had with Gary Daniels several months ago about his mom?"

Holly's mind immediately flashed to the argument. Gary Daniels didn't live in Cutler, but his mother Debbie did. She'd fallen and broken her hip several months ago, and Gary wanted to move her to a nursing home. Debbie was adamantly against it. She'd asked Holly to find a live-in nurse.

Gary had been incensed. He'd shown up at Holly's office and made a scene.

Aiden's mouth hardened. "He called you a few choice words and accused you of meddling in his family's business."

"Yes, but that was months ago. I haven't seen or heard from Gary since. Why would he attack me now?"

"I don't know. But I intend to find out."

FOUR

Holly was desperate for a shower and her soft bed. She settled behind the wheel of her sedan with a sigh. For a moment, she rested against the headrest. Her muscles ached and a headache was brewing at the base of her skull.

"Ten minutes. In ten minutes, I'll be home." She turned the key in the ignition and the car rumbled to life. Christmas music spilled from the speakers. Aiden's patrol SUV pulled around the side of the police department. He'd insisted on following her home, and while Holly considered the move overboard, she admittedly felt safer with him nearby.

If she wasn't careful, the police chief was going to slip right through her defenses. She'd done a good job of keeping him at arm's length so far. But tonight's attack had changed things. Aiden's protectiveness combined with the sweetness in his office battered at the edges of her convictions.

Holly waved at Aiden before pulling out of the parking lot. Her cell phone rang and Gram's name flashed across the dash. Holly answered using the Bluetooth. "Hi, Gram. What are you still doing up?"

"Oh, your grandfather and I were watching an old movie and time got away from us."

"One of those love stories," Pop interjected. "She wouldn't let me pick a Western."

Guilt flooded over Holly. Her grandparents were early risers and never stayed up past 10:30. They'd put the movie on because they were up worrying about her. She hadn't done a good enough job convincing them everything was all right.

"Where are you, Jolly Holly?" Pop asked, using the nickname he'd given her as a little girl. Hearing it now made her smile.

"I'm on my way home. Aiden is following me to make sure I get there all right."

"Aiden's a good egg. I was happy when he became police chief. Have to tell you, it makes me feel a lot better knowing he's on the case."

"Me too."

Holly stopped at a red light and glanced in the rearview mirror. Aiden's large form was visible in the truck behind her. He thought Gary could be behind the attacks on her. Was he right? It occurred to Holly that her grandparents could be a good source of information. They knew the inner workings of the town better than she did.

Holly sat up straighter in her seat. "Hey, Gram, remember when Debbie Daniels fell and broke her hip?"

"Funny you should mention that." Gram's voice filtered over the speakers. "It was part of the reason I was calling. I was thinking about who might want to hurt you and, I'm sorry to say, Debbie's son came to mind."

"Why?"

"Because of the house value. That horrible developer... what's his name?"

"Michael Fisher," Pop interjected.

"Yes, Michael. Anyway, he purchases properties and turns them into neighborhoods. The Daniels' home is on that huge plot of land. Michael's been after Debbie to sell for ages, but she won't do it. Gary, her son, is very upset about it." Gram paused to take a breath. "Now, Holly, normally I don't speak ill of people, but these are special circumstances. Gary has an alcohol problem. Maybe a drug one too. He's been after his mother's money for a long time. When Debbie fell down and broke her hip, Gary thought he could convince her to move into a nursing home. I believe his intentions were to sell the house."

Holly's mind raced with the new information. "Except I got in the way."

"Yes. And you keep getting in the way. Providing a live-in nurse, arranging for the church group to take Debbie to Bible study, and so forth. You've made it possible for her to stay in her home."

They talked a bit more, but Gram and Pop couldn't provide any additional information. They said their goodbyes.

Holly turned in to her neighborhood. She lived in an apartment above her grandparents' garage. The porch light was a welcome sight.

She got out of her car and met Aiden as he walked up

the driveway. She quickly relayed the information from her grandparents.

Aiden whistled. "Well, that gives him motive. Gary may think by getting rid of you, his mom will be forced to sell her house."

It was horrible to think about. Holly shivered in the crisp air and crossed her arms. "So

now what?"

"Gary lives in Houston. I'll contact the local police department and ask them to bring him in for questioning." Aiden gave her a reassuring smile and placed a hand on the small of her back. "Come on, it's late. And cold. Let's get you inside."

Holly nodded, trying not to notice how nice Aiden's touch felt. His aftershave was warm and woodsy. It teased her senses. Some part of her wanted to lean into him, but she resisted. She was just tired. That was all.

That was all she would allow it to be.

They climbed the steps to her home. Holly paused on the top stair. Her chest constricted. "Aiden, the door to my apartment is open."

He immediately moved in front of her, his hand dropping to the weapon at his side. "Stay behind me."

Holly didn't need to be told twice. She had no illusions of bravery.

Aiden stepped forward and she followed. He used a booted foot to ease the door open wider. His broad shoulders blocked her view for a moment, but then Aiden moved.

She gasped.

Her apartment had been ransacked. The Christmas tree next to the bay window lay on its side. Ornaments were shattered, the pieces scattered across her carpet. Pages were ripped out of books and tossed on the floor. Her throw pillows were destroyed, as well as her television. Several hack marks—possibly made by a knife—ripped the fabric of her armchair.

Holly stepped farther inside, horror sinking into her, colored by anger. Her home. Her beautiful home that she'd worked hard to make a happy place was wrecked. She swallowed past the lump in her throat and raised her gaze.

"Wait." Aiden turned, but it was too late. Holly had seen the words spray-painted on her wall.

Leave town or die.

FIVE

The next morning, Aiden guzzled coffee. Exhaustion seeped into his bones and his eyes felt gritty, but there was no time to rest. He had a criminal to find.

After discovering Holly's destroyed home, Aiden had brought her to his parents' ranch. The wide-open spaces and security system made it harder for someone to sneak on to the property without being noticed. Aiden had spent most of the night making calls and researching Gary Daniels.

Footsteps preceded Holly before she appeared in the doorway of the kitchen. Aiden's heart skipped a beat. He tried to temper the reaction, but there was little use. Something about the beautiful social worker got under his skin. There was a protectiveness, yes. But it was more than that. Holly made him yearn for a happy marriage and a family of his own. Those dreams were something Aiden had thought were long gone.

"Morning." Aiden poured Holly a cup of coffee. "How did you sleep?"

"Better than I expected." She smiled and took the cup he offered. Holly walked to the wide windows overlooking the ranch. "It's beautiful here. Where is everyone?"

"My parents and sister have already had breakfast and are out working."

She cast him a bashful glance. "I slept late."

"You needed the rest."

Aiden was pleased to see the dark circles under Holly's eyes from last night were gone as was the hard line of worry around her mouth. Bringing her to the ranch had been the right move for everyone.

He took another long sip of his coffee. "Before I forget, I spoke to your grandparents this morning. I managed to convince them it was better to stay on their vacation." It was safer this way. Aiden had a limited number of officers working for him. It would be a stretch to keep an officer stationed outside the Miller residence for their protection. "Your grandfather made me promise to call if anything changes."

"He told me. Thank you, Aiden." She tucked a silky curl behind her ear. "They deserve to celebrate their anniversary. Not to mention, I think it's safer for them there. After last night's break-in, I realized they may get caught in the crossfire."

Her brow creased with worry. Time to change the conversation. Holly needed a break from the stress. Aiden turned to the stove and opened the oven door. "Mom saved us some breakfast. I've been keeping it warm. Are you hungry?"

"Starved. And it smells delicious."

Aiden pulled out two plates filled with pancakes and

sausage. He grabbed the fruit plate from the fridge along with condiments. He joined Holly at the table and they said grace before spending a few minutes fixing their plates.

Holly drowned her pancakes in syrup before taking a bite. "Yum. This is amazing. Your mom did a great job." She eyed the spread laid out on the kitchen table. "Although I don't know if we can eat all of this. It's enough food for an army."

He laughed. "My mom likes feeding people. Oh, by the way, she asked me to give you a message. We're decorating the Christmas tree tonight. Mom wants you to join us."

Holly paused, her fork halfway to her mouth. "Oh...I don't want to crash a family gathering."

"You won't be. They'll be happy to have you." Aiden stabbed at a sausage. "I'm not much for tree decorating and all that, so it'll be better if you help."

"You don't like tree decorating? Or is Christmas the problem?"

Aiden was surprised she hadn't heard. The Cutler rumor mill must have a kink in it somewhere. Or, more likely, Holly had avoided engaging in it. He opened his mouth to explain but hesitated. Telling the story always made him feel foolish.

Holly wiped her mouth. "Never mind, Aiden. You don't have to explain."

"No, it's okay. I was engaged to a woman named Jane. I thought we were happy and in love, but..." He shrugged. "She left me standing at the altar on our wedding day. Turns out she was actually in love with one of my good friends. They ran off together one week later."

Holly winced. "Ouch. I'm sorry, Aiden. That must've been very painful."

"It wasn't a walk in the park, but I'm glad Jane decided to call things off before our wedding."

"Yes, but I'm sure it still hurt."

Something inside him unraveled. Holly got it. Exactly what he couldn't articulate in any good way with words. Logically, Aiden knew he was better off without Jane, but his heart had still been broken.

"Our wedding date was in early December," Aiden continued. "It's not really Christmas that's the issue. This time of year drums up bad memories."

"Understandable. I'll try to rein in my enthusiasm."

Aiden seriously doubted she could. Holly had started decorating before Thanksgiving. She sang Christmas songs in October. There was a bright red bow hanging from the front of her car, and she'd been wearing holiday sweaters for the last several weeks. Ugly ones with bells and reindeer and loud colors. Today's had a dancing Mrs. Claus on a deep green background.

"Don't bother holding back your love of Christmas on my account," Aiden said. "I've never met anyone more excited than you. Not even five-year-olds."

She laughed as a blush crept up her cheeks. "I know. I take it overboard, but Christmas was difficult when I was younger. My parents spent a lot of time fighting. They finally divorced when I was twelve, and after that, I spent time shuffling between houses. My parents started dating other people and those significant others rotated in and out. Last year was an utter disaster." She grew quiet for a moment. "I had Christmas at my house and invited both my parents. It was a special day and I wanted us together for dinner. Not...you know...for them to get back together, but one meal as a family. An hour of peace."

Aiden couldn't imagine not having Christmas dinner with his family. After church service, it was one of the things he treasured most about the holiday. "Seems reasonable to me."

"Not to them. It ended with a huge fight and dinner landed on the floor. I ate alone at a fast-food place."

The pain threading through her voice reached out and grabbed him. Aiden slipped his hand over hers. "I'm sorry."

Holly squeezed his hand. "Don't be. That night led me here."

"How so?"

"I knew things had to change. For me. The best holiday I've ever had was with my grandparents. I was sixteen and visiting Cutler. It was magical. The stores were all lit up, the amazing church service, the kindness between neighbors. It was all I could think about while eating that burger and fries last Christmas. I started looking for a job in town the next day."

Her joy for Christmas suddenly made sense. She was happy to be here, surrounded by people who shared her excitement.

It struck him then exactly what Holly had offered. She would curb her enthusiasm for the holiday to make things easier for him. Aiden wouldn't let that happen. He couldn't. Holly was already dealing with enough as it was.

"Listen, my family has been bugging me to get into the holiday spirit. And I have to admit, I've been something of a grinch for the last several years. But maybe it's time to change things, starting with the tree decorating." His mouth twitched. "You might even get me to sing a carol or two tonight."

She laughed. "If you aren't careful, I'll rope you into singing with the church choir for the Christmas festival."

The mirth melted from her expression. Probably because talking about the church choir had reminded her of the attack last night. Aiden's suspicions were confirmed when Holly asked, "Can you give me an update on where things stand with the case?"

He nodded. "The crime scene unit went through your apartment, but they didn't find any fingerprints or incriminating evidence. Chances are, the perpetrator wore gloves. None of the neighbors saw anything suspicious either."

Holly sagged against the chair and rubbed her forehead. "So we have nothing physical to connect Gary to the crimes. Maybe he's not the one who attacked me and broke into my apartment. We could be looking into the wrong person."

"I'm keeping all possibilities on the table. I don't want to focus solely on Gary, but right now, he's still my primary suspect. Your attacker escaped in a dark-colored truck last night. Gary has a black F-150 registered in his name."

She dropped her hand from her forehead. "Half the county drives a truck."

"It's not solid evidence, I'll give you that. But it's a starting place. Gary has also been in trouble with the law before. He's been arrested for domestic assault and some bar fights. None of the arrests resulted in jail time, but it does show a pattern of anger issues. I had the Houston Police Department check Gary's house. He wasn't home. A neighbor told them he left yesterday on a hunting trip. I've got officers tracking the alibi down. In the meantime, I want to speak to Gary's mom, but I need to tread lightly."

"What do you mean?"

"For starters, Gary could be innocent. I don't want to sully his name. Small-town talk and all that. Additionally, I don't want Mrs. Daniels to know we're investigating her son. She may tip him off—knowingly or unknowingly."

Holly nodded. "Yeah, I could see that. The minute you left, she'd be on the phone to Gary trying to find out if it's true."

"Exactly. That's where you come in."

"Me?"

"We could go and visit Mrs. Daniels together. She's a client of yours and it's reasonable to check in with her every now and then."

Holly pegged him with a look. "That's sneaky."

"A bit." Aiden picked up his coffee mug. "It's also the best way to get the information we need without raising alarm bells. Like I said, if Gary is innocent, I don't want to drag his name through the mud."

"No, neither do I. It's a good plan. Let's do it." She hesitated for a moment. "I have some other clients to check in with as well."

"We can go together. Until we know more about what's going on, my intention is to stick close to you."

If nothing else, having a police officer by Holly's side would deter the perpetrator from trying again. Last night's attack coupled with the break-in at Holly's home had left Aiden on edge. The perpetrator was either desperate or determined.

Both could be deadly.

SIX

Debbie Daniels lived a short distance from town on the main road in a two-story home. The front porch was swept and several plastic reindeer stood in the yard, but the property also held signs of neglect. Weeds crowded the flower beds, a fallen branch—probably dislodged during a thunderstorm—lay rotting near the driveway, and the barn looked ready to topple over if someone sneezed on it.

"I need to arrange for the yard-cleaning service to come out again." Holly shut the passenger-side door to Aiden's SUV. "They did a great job a few weeks ago."

"I'm not surprised the developer wants to buy this land." Aiden scanned the surrounding tree line. "It's prime real estate. Close enough to town but enough acreage to make into a neighborhood."

Was Aiden merely assessing the property, or watching for trouble? Holly had the feeling it was the latter. A shiver ran down her spine and she hugged her coat tighter, resisting the urge to glance over her shoulder. She was with Aiden. He wouldn't let anyone hurt her.

It sank in then how much trust she placed in the lawman. Relying on another person didn't come easily for Holly. She'd learned early on to take care of herself. There wasn't a choice since her parents placed both work and significant others above their own child.

Living near her grandparents and being in Cutler—even for such a short time—was changing her. Holly was learning to let others in and accept help.

Or maybe it was simply Aiden. His steadfast confidence and genuine kindness were a heady combination. Holly couldn't imagine what his ex-fiancée had been thinking. Someone like Aiden didn't come around every day.

Holly could understand not wanting to marry the wrong person—her parents were a prime example of what happened when you did—but she couldn't comprehend humiliating Aiden. Or lying about being in love with him.

What would it be like to be married to Aiden? She knew the answer instantly. Wonderful. He was caring and considerate. Handsome. A man of values and faith.

"Holly?" Aiden's brow creased.

Holly belatedly realized she'd been staring at him. She blinked, giving herself a mental shake. This was no time to be standing around listing Aiden's virtues. Or thinking about what it would be like to marry him. They weren't in a relationship, and she didn't want to be. There was too much at risk if things fell apart. Breakups were often nasty. She'd learned that lesson as a child too.

Holly blinked again. A blush heated her cheeks. "Sorry. I was lost in thought there for a minute."

"You sure you're okay?"

He stepped closer, his gaze drifting over her face. His

hand reached up and absently brushed a strand of hair from her cheek, revealing the scrapes from yesterday's attack. Her heart skipped a beat and butterflies rioted in her stomach.

"Maybe you hit your head harder than you thought." Aiden's intense gaze settled on hers. "We should take you to the hospital."

Oh, he was confirming all her earlier thoughts. Aiden would be a wonderful husband. Her blush deepened. "No, I'm fine. Really."

Aiden dropped his hand. "Are you sure?"

"Positive. I promise." She started for the house. Holly needed some distance between her and Aiden. "Let's go talk to Mrs. Daniels."

They climbed the front porch steps and Aiden rang the bell. Moments later, thumping and muffled footsteps filtered through the door before it opened.

"Holly, Aiden." Debbie's wrinkled face broke into a wide smile. She leaned heavily on a cane, favoring her left side. Her silver hair was tucked into a bun on the top of her head. She peered at them over the reading glasses perched on the end of her nose. "What a pleasant surprise."

Holly returned the older woman's smile. "Sorry to drop by without calling—"

"Hush now. You have no need to call first." Debbie backed away to open the door wider. "Come in out of the cold. Have you ever seen such an icy winter? Well maybe once when I was a little girl. We had snow, which, as you know, almost never happens."

Debbie kept talking a mile a minute as she escorted them to the living room. The space was small but homey. It was also very clean. The wood television stand gleamed and not a speck of dust lingered on the bookshelf. A Christmas tree sparkled in the corner.

"Can I get you anything to drink? Kasey visited earlier today and she made some delicious iced tea."

While studying to be a paramedic, Kasey had worked as Debbie's live-in nurse. The two women hit it off immediately, and Holly wasn't surprised they still visited from time to time.

"No, Mrs. Daniels." Holly took a seat on the couch next to Aiden. "Thank you for the offer, but I'm fine. Although Kasey's ice tea is wonderful."

"It is. That girl is like the daughter I never had. Just today, she cleaned my house and helped me put up the Christmas tree. I offered to pay her for her time, but she refused." Debbie settled into the leather recliner. "You know money is tight since she took the paramedic's job. The city doesn't pay well. I've been calling the mayor's office about it for months. A good girl like Kasey deserves to be paid a fair wage."

While Holly agreed Kasey should be paid fairly, she had to bite the inside of her cheek to keep from laughing. The mayor's secretary must groan every time Debbie's number flashed across the caller ID. The older woman was a chatterbox. Especially when she got riled up about something.

"Now then, enough about that." Debbie set her cane over her lap and focused on Holly. "I heard about the attack on you last night. I'm so sorry, dear. Are you okay?"

"I'm fine, Mrs. Daniels. How are you doing? How's your hip?"

"It's healing slowly. But I'm an old woman, Holly, and we have our aches and pains. No need to dwell on them when there are more important issues to discuss." She turned her steel-eyed gaze on Aiden. "I assume, young man, that you are doing everything to capture this...this...culprit. Land sakes, attacking a woman while walking to her car from church." She tsked. "I never. Must be someone traveling through from the city or a visitor in town. None of our residents would do anything like that."

"I'm doing everything possible, ma'am," Aiden said. "Rest assured I want to catch the man responsible more than anyone."

Debbie arched a brow and her gaze flickered from Aiden to Holly and back again. A smile played on her face. "Well now, I'm glad to hear it. It might not be such a bad thing if the two of you spend more time together. You'd make a lovely couple. Has anyone told you that before?"

Holly initially refused to look in Aiden's direction, but from the pleased expression on Debbie's face, she'd gotten the reaction she wanted. It was too much. Holly peeked at the police chief out of the corner of her eye. Aiden's face remained blank, but a blush crept up the back of his neck. Embarrassed because he only saw Holly as a friend? Or because his feelings were deeper and mirrored Holly's own?

For one second, Holly was tempted to throw caution to the wind and ask.

She didn't. They were here to accomplish something. Time to get to business. Holly focused back on Debbie. "Mrs. Daniels, I spoke to my grandmother last night and she reminded me that the developer in town—Michael Fisher—offered to buy your place."

"He sure did. Well, you know, he's adamant about it. Kept upping the offer. Why just the other day he was here, sitting right there on the couch, trying to convince me to sell. My son, Gary, wants to do it. But there's something about that man I don't trust."

"Gary?"

She laughed. "Oh no, dear. The developer, Michael."

"Gary doesn't want to keep the house for himself?" Aiden asked.

"I'm afraid not. My son has a business in Houston and a life there." Debbie scowled. "But I won't be run out of my home. I was born here and I intend to die here."

That confirmed what Holly's grandmother had told her. Gary was very interested in selling. And from what Debbie said, the developer was just as eager to buy.

Aiden leaned forward on the couch. "How long has Michael been trying to purchase the property?"

"Six months at least. It got worse after I broke my hip. Michael was downright persistent. But I won't sell to that man." Debbie's nose wrinkled, as if she'd smelled something foul. "He's...slimy. And I told him flat out that Holly was helping me stay right here. Buying my groceries, arranging for the yard service, and finding an at-home nurse for me."

Debbie smiled at Holly. "I couldn't have done it without you, dear."

"I'm glad to help."

Holly spared a glance at Aiden. She could practically see the wheels in his head turning. Maybe they were focused on the wrong man. Michael Fisher had a reason to want Holly out of the picture. Without her help, Gary could convince his mother to go into a nursing home and sell the house. Both men would benefit.

Debbie leaned forward and looked down at the basket next to her chair. Her mouth puckered as she picked up knitting needles. "Holly, would you do me a favor and run upstairs to my bedroom? I have extra yarn in the top right-hand side of my bureau. I keep meaning to bring it down, but my mind's not what it used to be."

Holly rose. "Of course."

"Thank you, dear. The stairs are difficult since I broke my hip."

"It's no trouble." She gave the older woman a smile and went up the stairs. Several of the doors were closed. One led to a bathroom, and there were two guest bedrooms as well. Holly went straight back to Mrs. Daniels's room at the end of the hallway.

A soft lavender comforter covered the four-poster bed. Photographs lined the bureau. Holly smiled at the one of Mrs. Daniels and her late husband on their wedding day. They both looked overwhelmingly happy.

She opened the right-hand drawer. Two packages of yarn in different colors rested on top of several knitting books.

"What are you doing?" a voice growled.

Holly gasped and spun, dropping the yarn on the floor. Her gaze shot to the man standing in the bedroom doorway. Gary. His mouth was hard with anger, dark brows drawn together in a fierce scowl. In his hand was a gun.

It was pointed straight at her.

SEVEN

Debbie kept talking about knitting and yarn. Aiden tried to sneak in a word or two, but it was fruitless. He would have to wait for Holly. She had a way of directing the conversation without being rude.

A floorboard creaked above Aiden's head. It was too heavy to have been made by Holly's petite form. He rose from the couch. "Ma'am, is someone else in the house?"

Debbie blinked at him, no doubt taken aback by his abrupt question. "My son—"

"Gary's here?" Aiden was halfway to the stairs before the words left his mouth. His hand dropped to his waist and he undid the button on his holster.

"He arrived last night," Debbie said. "Aiden, what's the matter?"

He barely registered her question as he took the stairs two at a time. Gary had verbally attacked Holly once before. He might've been the man who assaulted her outside the church. What would Gary's reaction be when he discovered Holly in his mother's home? Aiden didn't know, but he wasn't willing to wait to find out.

As he reached the second level, Gary came into view. The man was standing at the end of the hall, his body blocking a doorway. He held a gun.

Aiden's heart rate skyrocketed as he pulled his own weapon. "Cutler police. Gary, put your gun on the ground and your hands on your head. Now."

Gary half turned but was wise enough to lower his weapon to his side. His beady eyes narrowed. He was barefoot, wearing sweatpants and a T-shirt. Several days' worth of growth darkened his jaw and his hair was mussed. The strong scent of stale whiskey filled Aiden's nose, even from his position down the hall.

"I ain't doing nothin'." Gary glared at him. "This is my house."

Aiden wasn't getting into a debate with a man holding a handgun. Especially considering Gary could be still drunk. Sleeping it off didn't mean the alcohol was out of his system, and Holly's safety was the priority. "I said put the weapon on the ground. Slowly."

"Okay, okay." Gary bent and dropped his gun on the worn carpet before raising his hands in a classic sign of surrender. "Take it easy there, Chief. I woke from a nap and heard someone moving around inside my mom's bedroom. I thought we had an intruder."

The door to one of the spare bedrooms was open. That coupled with Gary's clothes and messy hair supported his statement.

Aiden lowered his own weapon but didn't holster it. He

kept his gaze on Gary. "Step back and sit on the bed. Holly, are you okay?"

"I'm fine."

Her voice carried, but Aiden caught the tremble buried inside it. He moved closer to the bedroom and Holly came into view. She was pale and her hands shook. Yarn littered the carpet.

A rush of anger flooded over Aiden, but he battled it back. There was no room for personal emotions now. He needed to keep his head and think like a lawman.

"Is everything okay up there?" Debbie's voice carried from the lower floor. "Aiden? Gary?"

"It's okay, Ma. Just a misunderstanding." Gary glared at Aiden. The bed sagged under the bulk of his weight. "I don't need to be treated like a criminal in my own home. I already told you, I thought Holly was an intruder. What are you two doin' here anyway?"

"We're visiting with your mother."

He snorted. "More like meddling." Gary twisted his head to set his blazing glare on Holly. Hatred bled off him. "I already told you to leave my mom alone. We don't need your meddling and we don't need your charity."

"Holly is helping your mother." Aiden stepped into Gary's line of sight, blocking the man's view of Holly. "It's her job. Not to mention, it's assistance your mother wants."

"Ma needs more help than Holly or anyone else can give her. She needs nurses watchin' over her. She's gettin' older and things are going to get worse. Ma can barely manage the stairs now. It's not safe for her here." Gary's mouth hardened. "Holly's interference is only making the move harder. For everyone."

Aiden thought Debbie should be free to stay in her home as long as possible. But he didn't get a vote in the matter. What was his purview were the attacks against Holly. Considering Gary's feelings about her, it would be prudent to have Holly leave the room.

Aiden didn't turn to look at her. He wasn't taking his eyes off Gary for a moment. "Holly, why don't you take the yarn downstairs to Mrs. Daniels? Reassure her everything is okay."

There was movement behind him. He sensed rather than saw Holly move toward the door. Aiden shifted his body to keep himself between her and Gary at all times. The other man seemed resigned to sitting on the bed. Still, Aiden wouldn't take any chances.

Once Holly had slipped from the room, Aiden holstered his weapon. He took a deep breath to shore up the last of his emotions. "When did you arrive in town, Gary?"

"Last night. What's it to you?"

"Holly was attacked yesterday. Know anything about that?"

His mouth flattened. "Sounds like you're accusing me of something."

"Then let's clear the air right now. Where were you between the hours of eight and midnight?"

Holly had been attacked around nine, but Aiden wanted to cover his bases. The man who'd hurt her had likely driven to her house to ransack it after the attack.

"I was at Dee's Tavern off the highway." Gary met his gaze. "From six until after two. You can ask half a dozen people there, including the owner."

"I intend to." Aiden studied Gary's expression carefully,

but there was no hint of deception. Just arrogance. Still, something nagged at him. A sense that Gary's alibi was almost too pat. Too easy.

Then again, Aiden could be off-base. He didn't like Gary. Never had. The man's verbal attack on Holly several months ago had only cemented that feeling. His behavior today exacerbated it.

But cases weren't built on emotions. They were made with facts and evidence. Unfortunately, Aiden was in short supply of those.

He rested his hands on his duty belt. "I didn't see your vehicle when I drove up."

"I parked it in the barn, like I always do."

"Still have the black F-150?"

Gary stifled a yawn. "Yep."

"Mind if I take a look at it?"

"Actually, I do. I don't like cops nosing around my stuff." Gary seemed to wrestle with some thought before sighing. He ran a hand through his messy hair. "I don't get it. Why would I attack Holly?"

"Because you're aiming to sell this house and the property. Holly keeps helping your mom, making it easier for her to stay in the house on her own, and that interferes with your plans."

Gary's mouth dropped. "That's..." He paused for a moment. "Well, I was going to say dumb, but I have to admit, you've got a point. Still, I wasn't the one who attacked her."

Gary sounded so convincing, Aiden was tempted to believe him. But something nagged at him. An internal warning Aiden couldn't—or wouldn't—dismiss.

"Listen, Chief, I won't lie about not liking Holly." Gary tugged on his T-shirt. "I was right mad when Ma changed her mind about going into a nursing home after breaking her hip. But I don't attack women."

His record would suggest otherwise. Gary had been arrested several times on domestic battery charges. Aiden kept his voice neutral. "The day you yelled at Holly, you were pretty heated. If I ask around, am I going to find out you have a temper problem?"

"Yeah, but that don't mean nothin'." Gary waved a hand as if dismissing an annoying fly. "Some ladies I've dated have purposefully tried to get me in trouble. And bar fights happen. That don't mean I would attack Holly. Yell at her, sure. But physically hurting her is different. My daddy taught me not to raise a hand to a woman."

"You pulled a gun on her."

"I done already told ya. I thought Holly was an intruder." Gary scratched his jaw. "Listen, if I wanted to get rid of Holly, shootin' her would be the fastest way. Easiest one too. I've got several hunting rifles Dad left me when he passed, and I'm an excellent shot."

Aiden arched his brows. "If you're trying to convince me that you haven't thought about hurting Holly, you're doing a bad job of it."

"I'm making a point. Attackin' her in a parking lot don't make any sense."

Aiden stiffened. "How did you know she was attacked in a parking lot?"

Gary blinked. "Ma told me. This morning over breakfast."

Was he lying? Debbie had known about the attack

when they spoke downstairs. It was conceivable she'd told her son. Still... "When Holly came up to get the yarn, you were sleeping. Now you're telling me you had breakfast with your mom. Which is it?"

"Both are. I came home from the tavern late. Went to bed. Ma woke me up shouting this morning to have breakfast. I ate with her and then went back to bed." Gary scoffed. "Would you like to know what we ate too?"

"Actually, yes."

"Scrambled eggs, bacon, and biscuits. Oh, and Ma made cream gravy. It's my favorite."

Gary rambled off the menu without hesitation. Another thing that would be silly to lie about. Aiden could simply confirm it with Debbie.

He bent down and retrieved Gary's gun from the carpet. Aiden made sure the safety was on. The weapon's grip was free of scratches or marks, and the metal was shiny. "This looks new."

"It is. I bought it yesterday." Gary arched his brows. "Like I said, why would I attack

Holly in the parking lot when I could just shoot her and be done with it?"

It was a good question. One Aiden didn't have an answer for. Yet.

"Not to mention," Gary continued. "Holly ain't the only one helping Ma. I'd have to

get rid of Kasey too. She's just as guilty of meddling as Holly is."

That was another good point. Kasey had been at the house this morning helping Debbie clean and decorate her Christmas tree. Getting rid of Holly wouldn't stop Kasey from coming by. Unless...unless Gary used the attack on Holly to threaten Kasey.

Had he ever threatened Kasey? It was something to ask.

Aiden straighten his shoulders. "You need to stay away from Holly. You threaten her in any way, Gary, and I'll arrest you. If you see her on the street, you cross to the other side. Do you understand me?"

Gary's jaw tightened, but he nodded sharply. Aiden handed him the gun. "Good. I'll be in touch."

Gary raised a hand to stop him from leaving. "I didn't have nothin' to do with the attack on Holly. But you should ask around, Chief. Someone like her, someone who meddles in other people's families, has a way of making folks mad. I'm not the only one who hates her."

Aiden's muscles tightened. "Got any names for me?"

"Naw, that you'll have to figure out for yourself." Gary smirked. "You're the one with the badge."

Aiden spun on his heel and went down the hall. His mind churned. What if Gary was telling the truth? If he wasn't the one responsible for attacking Holly...

Then who was?

EIGHT

"I can't think of a single person Gary could be talking about." Holly tucked her hands in the pockets of her jacket as she and Aiden strolled down Main Street.

They'd just come from visiting her last client of the day —a single mother with a young baby. Now they were headed for the coffee shop in the center of town. Kasey had texted in response to Aiden's request for a meeting. They'd arranged to talk at the coffee shop before Kasey's paramedic shift started.

Late afternoon sunshine warmed Holly's back but did little to erase the cold dread buried inside her. "I've been thinking about Gary's claim all day. Yes, I help families find services, but I wouldn't call that meddling. I only work with people who want my help. Other than Gary, I've never had anyone get mad at me for it."

Aiden frowned. "Gary could be lying. Casting suspicion on others would leave me chasing my tail."

"Or he could be telling the truth, and I'm the one who's blind. Obviously, someone in town wants me gone."

Aiden placed a hand on her elbow, forcing her to stop on the sidewalk. "There are lots of people who want you here. Don't let Gary get inside your head."

She shifted her stance, keeping her focus locked on her black flats. "The negative stuff is always easier to believe. Have you ever noticed that?"

He tucked a finger under her chin, lifting her face until her gaze met his. Warmth and affection mingled in his blue eyes along with something else. Something deeper. Something that made Holly's heart pick up speed.

"I have noticed that," Aiden said. "But from where I'm standing, you're excellent at your job. Reliable, compassionate, and patient. This town is fortunate to have you, and I'm glad you decided to move here."

Holly's chest constricted. Aiden had a way of making her feel valuable and worthy. She was a fool. There was no way to harness these runaway emotions for Aiden. She was falling for him. Had been falling for him for months, but she wouldn't let herself admit it.

Holly's gaze dropped to Aiden's mouth. An invisible thread tugged her closer to him. What would happen if she kissed him? Gave into her desire to step into his arms?

Heartbreak.

The answer whispered through her mind and stopped her cold. She stiffened.

Aiden sensed the shift in her body and dropped his hand. He took a step back. Then another.

"Sorry." His handsome mouth lifted in a smile that didn't reach his eyes. "That..." His gaze skittered away from hers. A flush heated the back of his neck. "That was inappropriate. We work together. We're friends."

He felt it too. This undercurrent of attraction rippling between them. Holly wasn't sure if that made things worse or better. She was scared of taking a leap into the unknown. Her parents' relationship had ended in disaster.

"I..." Holly didn't know how to explain the jumble of emotions tumbling inside her. "There's just a lot going on right now. Complicating matters between us doesn't seem smart."

He gave a sharp nod. "You're right."

Aiden fell into step beside her as they finished walking to the coffee shop. The line of his shoulders was rigid as was the set of his mouth. She'd hurt him.

Regret pinched at Holly, but before she could figure out what to say, they reached the Ground Bean.

Aiden opened the door for her. Holly murmured thanks and stepped inside. Jazz music played faintly over the shop's speakers, mingling with the sound of customers' voices, and the hiss of the expresso machine. The scent of blueberry scones drew her to the counter. Aiden followed.

They placed their orders. As Holly waited for her coffee order, Aiden placed a hand on the small of her back and bent close to her ear. "Michael Fisher is here. He's heading our way."

She turned and found herself face-to-face with the property developer. He was mid-thirties with the lean physique of a swimmer. Michael smiled broadly and the goatee on his chin shifted. "Aiden. Holly. Hi. It's good I ran into you."

"Hi, Michael." Aiden shook the other man's hand. "What can I do for you?"

"Well, I've heard rumors around town about the attack

on Holly last night." Michael's gaze landed on her. His smile dimmed, as a shadow of fake concern played across his features. "I'm very sorry, Holly, about what happened to you. We don't know each other well, but I would never wish anything harmful on someone."

Holly wasn't exactly sure what to make of the conversation, so she fell back on being polite. "Thank you, Michael."

He beamed at her. "Wonderful. Well, then I can expect the rumors running all over town to stop then, right?"

"Rumors?" Aiden asked. "What rumors?"

"That I'm somehow responsible for the attack against Holly." Michael adjusted the thousand-dollar watch on his wrist. "It's absurd. Why would I want to hurt her?"

Holly blinked. What on earth was he talking about? No one had accused him.... She inhaled sharply.

Gary. After they left, he must've called Michael. Were the two men working together as she suspected? Aiden had assigned officers to track down Gary's alibi, but they were waiting for the tavern to open at six.

Aiden settled his hands on his duty belt. "I can't discuss an ongoing investigation. However, no one has accused you of being responsible for the attack on Holly."

He didn't say it, but Holly heard the missing end of Aiden's sentence. Not yet. Michael must've too because his expression turned hard.

"I don't appreciate my name being dragged through the mud." Michael kept his voice low so others couldn't overhear and a faint smile plastered on his face. To anyone else in the coffee shop, it would appear they were having an amicable conversation. "I might be new in town, but I have friends in high places. You'd do well to remember that, Chief."

A shiver raced down Holly's spine. No wonder Debbie didn't like this man. Holly had a feeling she was looking at the real Michael Fisher. He was someone who would do anything necessary to get his way. Including attacking her.

"Are you threatening me?" Aiden arched his brows. "Because, if so, that's a crime."

Michael leaned back and widened his smile. "No, Chief. I'm merely giving you some advice. I do hope you take it." He shifted his gaze to Holly. "Both of you."

With that, he turned on his heel and marched out of the coffee shop. Holly watched him go with a mixture of shock and trepidation. "Did that really just happen? It was like something out of a gangster movie."

"I agree." Aiden picked up their coffee orders from the counter. "And it only raised my suspicions of him."

Holly collected their pastries and followed him to a table. "Do you think he and Gary are working together?"

"I do now. Both of them stand to benefit if Debbie sells her property." He jerked his chin as the bell over the coffee shop door opened. "There's Kasey."

Holly's friend hurried over, her soft-soled shoes squeaking on the tiled floor. Kasey appeared frazzled. Her jacket was hanging open and her shirt was untucked. She pulled out a chair. "Sorry I'm late. The water went out in my apartment complex. I had to heat bottled water just to clean up for work."

"That's terrible." Holly handed her a coffee and a scone. "Hope you don't mind. I ordered you something."

"You're the best." Kasey smiled before taking a long

sip of the coffee. "Ahh, that's good. No water meant I couldn't make coffee either. It's been a rough start to my day already." She glanced at Holly and shook her head. "What am I saying? Not having water at the apartment pales in comparison to what you're going through. I'm sorry."

"No, it's okay." Holly reached out and squeezed her friend's arm. "Nothing to apologize for. Thanks for meeting us before your shift."

"Of course. Speaking of, we'd better get down to business. I need to be at work in thirty minutes." Kasey's gaze shifted between Holly and Aiden. "What's going on?"

Aiden gave her a quick rundown of their morning and their suspicions about Gary. When he was done, Kasey sat back in her chair. "Wow. I mean, wow."

"Do you think Gary could be responsible?" Holly asked.

"It's possible. He was enraged when Debbie refused to move after she broke her hip. Gary is something of a momma's boy, so he shifted his frustration to you. Kept saying you should mind your own business." Kasey bit her lip. "Holly, if I had known—"

"It's okay. He threatened me at my office a few months ago, remember? I didn't take him seriously either. I thought he was blowing off steam."

"Me too." She tugged on her silky ponytail. "Maybe we were both wrong."

Aiden leaned on the table. "Has Gary ever threatened you, Kasey?"

"Not directly. He's...not friendly." She shrugged. "He tolerates me. That's the best way to describe it. Debbie and

I are close, and Gary knows it. He's careful to walk a fine line so I don't say anything to his mom."

Holly considered her friend's assertion. It made sense. Kasey did a lot for Debbie, including keeping her company. Gary could be taking things one step at a time. Getting rid of Holly would be the easier option. Then Gary could use those attacks to threaten Kasey to back off naturally. His mother would be none the wiser.

"How close is Gary with Michael Fisher?" Aiden asked.

Kasey frowned. "They're friendly, but I think it's business more than a genuine bond. Michael is hoping Gary will convince his mom to move. Why are you asking?"

"Gary may have an alibi for last night. We're looking into it, but I wondered if he might be working with someone."

"With Michael, no. Now his cousin...that's a different story."

Holly's hand tightened on her cup. "His cousin?"

"Eddie Daniels."

The name was familiar. Holly had the vague image of a dark-haired man with a handlebar mustache. "Mrs. Daniels has a photograph of him on her bookshelf."

Kasey nodded. "He and Gary are business partners as well as cousins. I've only met Eddie a handful of times, but I didn't like him." Kasey shuddered. "Eddie creeps me out."

"Can you elaborate?" Aiden asked.

"Not really. It's more like a feeling. He hasn't done anything specific, but sometimes you meet someone and you just don't like them." She glanced at her watch and sighed. "Sorry, guys, I gotta run. Wish I could've been more helpful."

"You've been very helpful."

They walked out of the coffee shop together. The sun had set behind the trees, and the temperature was dropping quickly, but the crisp air felt good in Holly's lungs. Her breath puffed out in front of her.

Kasey adjusted her scarf before hugging Holly. "Thanks again for the coffee and the treat. Let me know if there's anything else I can do."

"I will, thanks." She smiled at her friend. "Have a great night at work."

"I'll try. Bye, Aiden."

With a last wave, Kasey turned and headed for her vehicle. Holly fell into step beside Aiden as they headed for his patrol car. "What do you think?"

"I think our suspect list keeps getting longer. I—"

Something whizzed past Holly and landed in the wall of the building near her. Pieces of brick sprayed out.

"Get down!" Aiden lunged in Holly's direction.

Several more pops echoed. Aiden wrapped his arms around her. They tumbled to the ground. The air whooshed out of Holly's lungs. Witnesses screamed down the street as glass on Aiden's patrol car exploded.

Someone was shooting at them.

NINE

Hours later, Aiden winced as the doctor secured a bandage to his arm. A bullet had grazed him and it'd taken fifteen stitches to close the wound. His head was aching, his body sore, and his mood foul. But Holly was unharmed.

In the end, that's what mattered.

"I'm writing a prescription for antibiotics." The doctor scribbled on a pad while reciting a quick round of wound-care instructions. "Come back if you start to run a temperature. The nurse will be in with discharge paperwork shortly."

Aiden took the prescription from her. "Thanks, doc. Would you mind telling the officer in the waiting room to come on back."

"Not at all, Chief."

She left. Aiden reached for his shirt. It was an extra one from his go-bag in the SUV. The original shirt had been destroyed by the bullet and blood. He gingerly slipped his injured arm through before quickly working the buttons.

s numb for the moment, but Aiden had little ing to be in pain later on.

 the hospital room swung open and Holly as followed by Officer David Carpenter. David was one of Aiden's best men. Solid, dependable, and smart. He'd been the lead investigator on Holly's attack since Aiden had spent most of his time guarding her safety.

Not that he was doing a very good job of it.

"How are you?" Holly rushed to Aiden's side. She embraced him.

The familiar scent of her vanilla shampoo teased Aiden's senses. He hugged her back, doing his level best to ignore how good she felt in his arms. Holly considered him a friend. Nothing more. That was painfully obvious today when Aiden had almost kissed her.

"I'm fine, Holly." He released her, and she stepped back. "The wound looked worse than it actually was."

It'd bled quite a bit and running after the individual taking potshots at them had made things worse. Unfortunately, the shooter managed to escape.

Aiden turned his attention to David. "Where do things stand?"

"Gary Daniels's alibi fell through." David pulled out a notebook from his pocket and flipped it open to read from his notes. "He arrived at Dee's Tavern at six as he claimed but disappeared around eight thirty. For an hour, no one saw him. Then the bartender remembered serving him a new whiskey at half-past nine."

"That's very specific. The tavern gets busy most evenings around that time."

David nodded. "She remembered because Gary tipped her very well."

"That explains it." Aiden caught Holly's confused expression. "Gary wanted to make sure she recalled serving him. He was setting up the alibi. But there's a forty-five-minute gap where Gary was missing from the bar. That's more than enough time to drive to the church and attack you."

"But it's not enough for him to have attacked me and also trashed my apartment."

Aiden considered her point. "True. We could be dealing with two people. One attacked you at the church, another trashed your apartment. Gary is probably working with someone, but we can't know for sure until we interview him again."

David rocked back on his heels. "Problem is, Gary's missing. He left his mother's house shortly after y'all talked to him this morning, and no one has seen him since. Officers from the Houston Police Department are watching his house. I've also got a BOLO out for his truck."

"What about his cousin? Eddie Daniels."

David whistled. "Yeah, that guy is a piece of work. Arrested multiple times for various crimes ranging from assault to theft. He spent some time in the county jail, but that was years ago. He and Gary own and operate a construction business. I pulled the financials. It's hurting for money. We've tried to locate Eddie, but guess what?"

"He's missing too."

"You got it."

Aiden clenched his jaw. "They could be working

together. Do you have a BOLO out for vehicles registered in Eddie's name?"

David nodded. "I've also followed up with Mrs. Daniels. She gave us permission to look in her late husband's gun safe. A rifle is missing along with several boxes of ammunition. The brand is consistent with the shells recovered from the scene of the shooting. The lab will run additional tests, but we'll have to wait a few days for them."

"Eddie may not be the only one Gary is working with. Michael Fisher could be involved. He saw us at the coffee shop and could've passed our location on to either Eddie or Gary. Or both." Aiden's mind spun with the various possibilities. "Do a deeper background check on Michael for me."

David nodded. "You looking for anything in particular?"

"Close ties to either of the Daniels men, for starters. Kasey said Michael and Gary were friendly, but she didn't consider them close."

"They all lived in Houston," Holly said.

Aiden frowned. "Come again?"

"Before moving to Cutler, Michael was working in Houston. He told me so when I first met him. I don't remember the name of the real estate company he was working with, but Gary and Eddie are in construction." She shrugged. "Maybe their paths crossed there."

David made a note on his pad. "I'll look into it."

The door opened and a nurse entered. She was carrying a tablet and some paperwork. "Excuse me, I have your discharge papers."

David promised to be in touch if anything new developed and left. Aiden went through the hospital paperwork, but his mind was only half on it. The other half was mulling the case.

After the nurse bustled out, Holly turned to him. "What's bugging you?"

Aiden should've been surprised at Holly's question, but he wasn't. She was observant. And she had a knack for reading people's emotions. He folded the paperwork the nurse had given him. "It's something Gary told me during our conversation."

Aiden hesitated. He didn't want to upset Holly any more than she already was. The woman was strong, but in the last two days, she'd been attacked, had her home broken into, and been shot at.

She arched her brows. "Don't hold back on my account, Aiden. I can take it."

He sighed. "Gary made the argument that attacking you in the parking lot was pointless. If he'd wanted to hurt you, he'd shoot you and be done with it."

Holly tilted her head. "He told you what he was going to do."

"Right, but why didn't he do it in the parking lot last night? Why shoot you today? It doesn't make sense." Aiden rubbed his forehead. "Maybe I'm overthinking it. Gary could've been just smug. He knew what he was going to do and told me so."

"You aren't overthinking it. It's weird. Maybe Gary isn't the one behind all of this. Maybe Eddie is working on his own."

"And Gary knows about it? Possibly. If that's true, then Gary could be in danger himself."

"Is your head hurting?" Holly dipped her head to catch his gaze. "Do you need some pain medication?"

He forced a smile. "No, I'll take some later. Let's get out of here. There's a Christmas tree to decorate."

"Your mom was going to postpone—"

"Not a chance." Aiden placed his hands on Holly's shoulders. "We need a break. A few hours of hot cocoa and tree decorating. Maybe a carol or two."

Her mouth twitched. "You're teasing me. You have no intention of singing carols. It'll ruin the Grinch thing you have going."

He winked. "Even the Grinch was reformed, Holly. Suppose I can be too."

Aiden's personal vehicle was parked in the hospital lot. An officer had dropped it off earlier since the patrol SUV was going to need repairs after being shot at. Holly offered to drive and Aiden took her up on it. His arm was starting to throb and his headache was growing.

Aiden popped some pain medication at home. Then, for the next several hours, he made a conscious effort to forget the outside world. Not for himself, although it was a welcome break. No, he did it for Holly. She needed to dive into the holiday cheer. Making cocoa, setting out decorations, oohing and ahhing over his mother's ornament collection. It brought a smile to her face and erased the tension in her back.

Holly was beautiful. Not just her pretty face or the wild mane of hair. It was her inner beauty that reached inside Aiden and wouldn't let go.

Lord, I know Holly needs my protection and that's why she's in my life. But why do I have these feelings for her that I can't get rid of?

And he did have feelings for her. Those emotions ran deeper than Aiden wanted to admit. The recent attacks on Holly had forced him to face them. Their near kiss had been a long time coming.

And the more Aiden thought about it, the more confusing it became. He could've sworn Holly was about to kiss him too. Had he really misinterpreted all her touches? The soft looks she gave him? Or was something else going on?

The only way to find out was by asking.

Gradually as the evening wore on, the living room emptied out. His sister went home. His parents retired to bed. Aiden made fresh cups of cocoa and handed one to Holly. She was nestled on the end of the sofa, studying the Christmas tree lights.

"We did a good job, don't you think?" She smiled. "And you've been holding out on me, Aiden James. You can sing."

He chuckled and pegged her with a look. "Don't even think about it. I'm not joining the church choir."

"Shame." She giggled. "You have cocoa on your lip."

Holly reached over and ran her thumb across his mouth. Aiden's breath hitched. The air circling them became charged, and he expected her to back away. She didn't.

"Aiden...I owe you an apology."

He blinked. Aiden wasn't sure what he'd expected her to say, but it wasn't that. "Why on earth do you owe me an apology?"

"Because I panicked this afternoon." Her thumb slid

from his mouth down the line of his cheek and then his jaw. The touch left molten heat in its wake. "I hurt you and I didn't mean to."

"What's going on, Holly?" He set his cocoa on the coffee table and turned to face her straight on. Aiden took her hand, sliding her fingers through his. "I don't understand, but I want to."

She took a deep breath. "I'm scared."

"I know. These last two days have been—"

"No, not about the attacker." She paused and her brow wrinkled. "I mean, yes, I'm scared about the maniac shooting at me, but that's not what I'm talking about now."

Aiden was quiet, letting her sort out her thoughts.

Holly took another deep breath. "I'm worried about us. About starting a relationship with you because I don't know what will happen if things don't work out. What if you hate me? What if we can't stand each other?" She searched his face. "My parents...they must've been in love at some point. Until it all fell apart."

Aiden squeezed her hand gently. He understood her fears. Holly's heart had been broken. In a different way than Aiden's, but he knew better than anyone, the hurt left scars.

"Holly, I won't make promises to you that I can't keep. What I do know for certain is that we would never end up like your parents. We're different from them." He paused. "You're different from them. You think with your heart and don't hold grudges."

Tears flooded her eyes. They shattered him. Aiden cupped her face in his hands. "I could never hate you, sweetheart. Never."

Her lip trembled. "You say that now...but..."

"I know. It's hard." He swiped the water from her face with the pad of his thumb. "The negative stuff is always easier to believe."

She nodded. "When those shots rang out...when I saw you were bleeding, I kept thinking over and over again that I hadn't been honest with you. I hadn't told you the truth and I was afraid I would never get to."

"Tell me now."

"I have feelings for you, Aiden. I've had them for a long time. And they're scary and I have doubts and I don't know what to do about it." She sniffed. "I'm a mess."

"No, you're being honest." He brushed a lock of hair off her forehead and tucked it behind her ear. "I have feelings for you, too, Holly. Deep ones. But you're not ready to move forward. That's okay. All I ask is that you pray about it. Keep an open heart and give me a chance to convince you this can work."

She smiled softly. "I will."

Holly leaned closer and brushed her mouth across his. Aiden's heart skittered and then took off like a bullet. Heat flooded his veins. He pulled her closer and deepened the kiss. Everything about this woman moved him. She was kind and generous. Honest and caring. His hands dipped into her hair and got tangled in the strands. He poured all his feelings into each touch, each caress of his mouth.

His phone rang. Aiden broke off the kiss with a groan. "I wish I could ignore that."

Holly laughed, but her cheeks were flushed. Whatever Aiden was feeling, she shared it. There was hope for them. Right now, it was enough.

Aiden pulled the phone from his belt and answered it. "Chief James."

"Aiden, it's Debbie Daniels. I have information about the attacks against Holly. You and Holly need to see it. Tonight."

TEN

The headlights of Aiden's truck cut through the night. Holly stayed within the speed limit, but it was hard. She gripped the steering wheel. The warmth and joy from an evening spent with Aiden's family had fled, leaving a cold pit in her stomach. What had Debbie uncovered?

She glanced at Aiden in the passenger seat. He was rubbing his forehead as though a headache was brewing. Probably was. He'd asked her to drive, which was proof enough he was in pain. Her heart ached. Aiden was in this mess because of her. Yes, it was his job, but he could've died protecting her today.

She didn't want to think about that. Losing Aiden...the idea stole her breath. Their kiss had only cemented her feelings. It also increased her fears. Holly didn't want to think about that either. She'd been honest with Aiden and that was enough for the moment. There was too much happening to tackle a deeper dive into her insecurities about love.

"Slow down, Holly." Aiden pointed to a vehicle on the

side of the road. "Let me say hi to Officer Jacks. He's watching the Daniels house in case Gary or his cousin Eddie arrive."

Holly did as Aiden asked. She didn't bother pulling over onto the side the road. Traffic was almost nonexistent given the late hour.

Officer Ben Jacks heaved himself out of the patrol car. He was short and barrel-chested, with thinning hair and a steady-eyed gaze. Holly had interacted with him several times. He was patient and thorough.

Aiden rolled down his window and frigid air blew in. "Hi, Ben."

"Howdy, Chief." Ben nodded in Holly's direction. "Ma'am."

"Anything new to report?" Aiden asked.

"No, sir. Everything's been quiet." Ben frowned. "Late for a visit, ain't it?"

"Mrs. Daniels called and asked us to come by. She said it's important. Keep a close eye on the house while we're there."

He stiffened. "Of course. It's my job."

Aiden held up his hand. "No disrespect intended, Ben. We were shot at earlier today and I'm not sure how the perpetrator knew where we were. Just advising extra caution, that's all."

The other man's shoulders dropped. "Understood. Don't worry, sir. I've got your back."

"I know you do." Aiden reached out to shake his officer's hand. "Thanks."

They said their goodbyes to Ben, and Holly continued up the winding drive to the Daniels' home. Lights inside the house blazed. Debbie must've been watching for them from the window because she opened the front door before Holly exited the vehicle.

"I'm so glad you're here." Debbie waved them inside and shut the door. Her hair was in rollers and she wore a robe and slippers. She leaned on her cane. "Thanks for coming out so late. I wouldn't be able to sleep a wink until I showed you what I'd uncovered."

"We're all ears, Mrs. Daniels." Aiden took his position on the couch. Holly joined him.

"Well, I have a friend whose son is a hacker. They call him a white hat, but he doesn't actually wear a hat." She flapped her hand. "It's all very confusing."

Despite the seriousness of the situation, Holly had to smother a smile. Debbie had also piqued her curiosity. White hat hackers were normally hired by companies to test security systems for vulnerabilities and then to shore up those weak spots.

"Anyway, my friend's son is excellent with computers," Debbie continued. "When Michael Fisher wanted to purchase my land, I had him looked into."

Holly's mouth dropped open. "You ran a background check on Michael?"

"Of course, dear. I'm not doing business with a man unless I know he's on the up-and-up. Besides, I told you there was something about him I didn't like. He's sleezy." She rose up as much as her healing hip and arthritic spine would allow. "Turns out I was right."

Debbie hobbled over the bookshelf and pulled down a file folder. "Michael Fisher isn't actually his real name. It's Harry Sterling. He's a prime suspect in several operations targeting elderly people. Fishing schemes and that sort of thing."

Aiden rose from the couch and took the folder from Debbie. He opened it and flipped through the papers. Holly read over his shoulder. There were photographs, arrest records, and descriptions of the schemes used to defraud victims of their money.

It made Holly's head spin. "I don't understand. If Michael is really this guy Harry, why would he want to buy this property? That doesn't match any of the schemes he's run in the past."

"Because it's the beginning of one." Aiden's hand tightened on the file folder. "He buys the land here for a cheap price. It creates a record of ownership. Then he creates a mock-up of homes and starts selling them to prospective buyers. He gets their down payment, maybe he builds one or two, but then he keeps re-selling the plots of land over and over again without actually building anything. He works fast before people can put the pieces together. By the time people realize they've been defrauded, Michael is long gone."

Debbie humphed. "Rotten man."

"Okay, let's say you're right, Aiden. Mrs. Daniels refused to sell her land. Why didn't Michael purchase something else?"

"I'm not sure. Maybe because of the location of this property. It would make the plots easier to sell at a higher price since it's close to town."

There was something more he wasn't saying. It took Holly a few moments to figure out why.

Michael could be working with Gary and Eddie. The

Daniels owned a construction business. If Michael wanted to make it look like he was building houses, Gary and Eddie would prove valuable.

But, of course, Aiden wouldn't besmirch Gary to his mother without solid proof. It was kind and considerate. It was also logical. How much had Mrs. Daniels told Gary about her investigation into Michael?

Aiden must've been following her chain of thought because he leaned forward. "Mrs. Daniels, who have you talked to about the background check?"

"Only my friend and her son. And now you two."

"Not Gary? Not any neighbors or family members?"

She shook her head and the rollers bobbed. "No, I didn't want to tell Gary until after I had proof. He's so enamored with Michael. That man managed to convince my son he's successful. The fancy watch, the nice car, and expensive clothes. It's deceptive."

Debbie's comments only reinforced Holly's suspicion that the men might be working together.

"Listen, Aiden, I know you suspect Gary is involved in this." Debbie leaned on her cane and settled into the recliner. "I won't deny my boy has some issues. He drinks too much and he's been in trouble with the law. His daddy's death was hard on him. But Gary is a good man. He wouldn't hurt Holly."

Was Debbie right? Was her son innocent in all this? Or was he one of the perpetrators?

It was hard to know. There were too many people involved, and clearly Holly had stumbled into something unknowingly. At the same time, she was grateful. If the men hadn't targeted Holly, would they have hurt Debbie for continuing to refuse to sell the property? Gary might not kill his mother, but Michael was a different story.

In fact...it made sense. If the men were working together, Michael might have been getting impatient. Gary could've decided to remove Holly from the picture to speed things up and force his mother to sell.

But if Holly and Aiden persisted, would Mrs. Daniels become the target?

Once Aiden and Holly were back in his vehicle, she explained her theory and posed the same question to him.

Aiden frowned. "That's a good thought. I already have Officer Jacks keeping an eye on the house covertly in case Eddie or Gary circle back around. I'll tell him to make his presence known. That should deter an attack on Mrs. Daniels. Michael wouldn't be bold enough to hurt her with an officer nearby."

"Someone was brazen enough to shoot at us."

"Yes, but I suspect that was either Gary or Eddie. Based on Michael's criminal history, he doesn't like to get his hands dirty."

She sent up a silent prayer that Aiden was right and asked the Lord to watch over Mrs. Daniels. She pulled out of the driveway and onto the two-lane country road. Holly popped on her brights. The road was dark, and deer were notorious for crossing at night.

Aiden made a few phone calls. Holly listened with half an ear, her mind still twisting with the new information Debbie had provided. Which men were involved? How deeply? Was it possible Gary and Eddie were also victims of Michael's smooth-talking ways? Holly supposed it was feasible. Money and success could be blinding.

Aiden straightened in the seat next to her, his gaze locked on the sideview mirror. "We're being followed."

Holly tightened her grip on the steering wheel. She wasn't sure if Aiden was talking to her or the person on the phone. She glanced at the rearview mirror.

Light flooded the interior of the vehicle, bouncing off the mirror and straight into Holly's eyes. A truck engine roared behind them.

"Hold on!" Aiden shouted.

Holly screamed as the truck rammed into the back of their vehicle. Her heart rate spiked and she punched the gas, desperate to put some distance between the cars.

"Breathe, Holly. Help is coming." Aiden was spouting words into his phone at a clipped rate. His weapon was already in his hand. The window was down. Frigid air blew in, whipping her hair in her face. "You're doing great, Holly. Steady now."

She barely heard him. The road curved ahead of them and she was going too fast. The truck roared again.

It slammed into their bumper and the SUV skidded. Holly's seat belt tightened and she tried her best to turn into the spin but everything was moving too fast. Trees whirled in a frantic pace beyond the windshield.

They were going to crash.

ELEVEN

The next evening, Aiden leaned against the wall and watched as the church choir members warmed up in preparation for their performance at the Cutler Christmas Festival. Holly was smack-dab in the center. Her hair was pinned back from her face in a soft wave that drew attention to her high cheekbones. From the outside, she looked like a woman without a care in the world.

He knew better. Last night's car accident had been a close call. His personal vehicle was banged up but drivable. It'd ended up in a ditch thanks to Holly's quick thinking and good driving skills. The truck following them had roared off before Aiden could get a license plate.

Twenty-four hours later and the three prime suspects in the attack were missing. No one had seen Gary, Eddie, or Michael. Aiden suspected the men were hiding out together. They had to be close. But where? He didn't have an answer. It was incredibly frustrating.

The choir finished their warm-up and Holly beelined

for him. Her cheeks were flushed and a spark brightened her eyes. "How did it sound?"

"Gorgeous." Her happiness was infectious, and Aiden found himself smiling in return. "I think this year's celebration will be the best one yet."

"You do? Really? Or are you just saying that to make me feel better?"

"I believe it." He winked. "But I'm admittedly biased. I have a huge crush on one of the sopranos."

She laughed and rose on her tiptoes. Her lips brushed against his cheek and it sent a wave of warmth through him. "Thank you, Aiden. For supporting me. I know my participation in the celebration makes you nervous."

It did. They'd had several conversations about it today, but in the end, Holly decided it was best to keep her word. Aiden understood why. The celebration benefitted the Cutler Fund, which Holly used for her clients. People like Mrs. Daniels, who wanted to stay in their home but needed extra assistance. Single mothers struggling to pay for childcare. Families dealing with unexpected sickness and high medical bills.

The work Holly did changed lives. It was important. And the money raised tonight would make a difference.

Aiden wrapped his arm around her waist. "We've got officers stationed throughout the crowd. I called in extra assistance from the state police as well."

He'd done everything by the book, but there were no guarantees. Only God could provide that. So, Aiden did everything within his control and gave the rest to the Lord.

Aiden tapped Holly's nose. "All you need to worry about is your solo."

She wrapped her arms around his waist and laid her head on his chest. He held her, taking a quiet moment for himself. He kissed the top of her head. "You okay?"

She leaned her head back until she could look him in the eye. "More than okay. And it's thanks to you. It might sound strange, but if my life is going to be threatened, there's no one else I'd rather have protecting me."

"That's..." His chest swelled with an indescribable emotion. "That's quite possibly one of the nicest things anyone has ever said to me."

Holly laughed. "I need to pay you more compliments then."

The room had emptied out, the rest of the choir assembling outside for the tree lighting service and celebration. Aiden and Holly were alone. He took the private moment to steal a kiss. Then another.

When Holly stepped out of his arms, her cheeks were flushed again. "Come on, Chief. There's a crowd waiting, and if you keep kissing me like that, I'll never make it to the celebration."

She slipped her hand into his and Aiden interlocked their fingers. They stepped out into the chilly night air. People mingled across the street in the square. An unlit Christmas tree sat ready and waiting. Children played inside the bouncy houses. Stands with various tasty treats lined the church parking lot. The scent of cinnamon and chocolate carried in the air.

The choir was assembling on bleachers set up near the tree. Holly squeezed his hand. "I'd better go. It looks like things are about to start."

"Be careful. And break a leg."

She kissed his cheek again. "After the celebration tonight, do you think we could talk? About us?"

Joy burst in his chest. Had Holly made her decision about their relationship? It sounded like it. Aiden wanted to tug her back inside the church and have the conversation right away, but there was no time. Instead, he nodded.

Holly bounced down the stairs and crossed the street. He watched her go, a lump in his throat. The kisses they'd shared took on a new meaning. Aiden had visions of engagement and marriage dancing through his head. But a nugget of worry wormed its way through his happy thoughts.

His ex. He'd thought Jane was in love with him too. They'd shared kisses, dated, and had—what he thought—was a genuine friendship. It'd been a lie.

Was the relationship with Holly a lie too? Maybe she was pretending to keep from hurting his feelings, and later tonight she would tell him there was no future for them?

Those fears grew with every step Aiden took across the square to his position near the choir. He'd already staked out a spot enabling him to watch Holly and keep an eye on the crowd. Aiden buried his concerns and emotions behind a wall of professionalism. There was nothing he could do about his relationship with Holly at the moment. Now, his mission was to keep her safe.

For the next twenty minutes, the choir sang different carols. The mayor spoke a few words. The switch was flipped on the tree lights and a collective gasp went up from the crowd at the beauty. Aiden felt someone's gaze on him. He turned and caught Holly's eye. She smiled brightly. Her hair was lit up by the Christmas lights.

He loved her. Aiden couldn't deny it. The very idea of

losing her... He couldn't. He didn't want to. But it wasn't up to him. Holly had to decide to step forward into their love. She had to want it as badly as he did.

He could only pray she would.

The crowd started to disperse. A scream echoed out. It sent Aiden's heart into overdrive. The cry hadn't come from Holly but from a woman close to Aiden. Still, he couldn't see the trouble.

He started weaving his way through the crowd. "Police. Out of the way. Police."

Aiden broke through a circle of people. An elderly woman lay on the ground, tears streaming down her wrinkled face. She wasn't familiar to him. A visitor from a nearby town, perhaps?

"Ma'am, is everything okay?" Aiden bent down. "Are you injured?"

"My elbow. It might be broken."

"What happened?"

"Someone rushed me and stole my purse. Came out of nowhere right after the tree was lit. I was distracted. Next thing I know, I was pushed to the ground."

A distraction. Panic rushed over Aiden.

Holly.

Two other officers arrived as Aiden sprang to his feet. He pointed to the woman on the ground. "Help her."

Aiden spun on his heel, racing back toward the choir. "Holly!"

She wasn't where he'd seen her last. Aiden grabbed a choir member. "Where's Holly?"

"She was right over there."

He looked to see where the woman pointed. Holly

wasn't there either. Aiden called in for assistance on his portable radio. Then he grabbed nearby choir members and asked for their assistance in the search. Every motion was frantic and rushed. He clung to the hope she was somewhere in the crowd, but in his heart, Aiden already knew. He'd messed up.

Holly was gone.

TWELVE

Holly moaned.

Pain reverberated in her head. Her shoulder was aching and her arm numb. She attempted to shift positions, but her body wouldn't cooperate. Her hands were secured together. It smelled faintly of motor oil and sweat.

Holly pried her eyes open, fighting the darkness and a swell of nausea. Weak light poured in above her head. The floor rocked beneath her. Holly struggled to make sense of what she was seeing. White panels with strange indentions. Tool boxes and a handsaw. Was she...was she inside an industrial van?

Her heart picked up speed as flashes of memory sparked in her mind. The tree lighting service. A scream from the crowd. Aiden had disappeared from view, running to provide aid. Holly remembered saying a prayer and then pain exploded in her head.

Someone had attacked her. Hit her over the head while Aiden and everyone else was distracted by the scream and then placed her in some kind of delivery van. There had been dozens of vendors at the Cutler Christmas Festival, selling food and sweets. An unmarked delivery van wouldn't have struck anyone as strange.

Who was driving? She craned her head, but the front of the vehicle was blocked. She fumbled with the restraints around her wrists. Her fingers brushed against metal. Handcuffs. One glance confirmed her suspicion. Holly's questions multiplied as her confusion deepened. Was someone in the police department behind this? Officer Carpenter? Or Officer Jacks?

The vehicle bounced. Holly's head whacked against the hard floor and a fresh wave of pain washed over her. She groaned. Her eyes were heavy and it was a struggle to remain conscious. But she had to. There was no choice. The driver was taking her somewhere, and Holly could only imagine, things would get worse for her once they arrived at the destination.

Lord, please. Give me strength. Walk me through this.

It would take time, but Aiden would realize Holly was missing from the celebration. He would be looking for her.

Unbidden tears sprang to her eyes. What if she never saw Aiden again?

Holly bit her lip and blinked the tears back. She couldn't think about Aiden or her regrets. Her focus needed to be on staying alive. Every minute she delayed gave the police another minute to locate her. Her gaze swept the van again. Most of the items were too big to hide or use in her weakened state. But a lone screwdriver stuck out from an improperly closed toolbox.

That. It could be used as a weapon. Holly scooted her body across the van floor, ignoring the agony ripping through her skull. She positioned herself within reach of the screwdriver. Fortunately, her hands were handcuffed in front of her body. But from the angle of her position, she couldn't see what she was doing.

The van slowed and turned. It didn't pick up speed again. Wherever they were going, it was close.

Panic swelled. Holly took a deep breath to counteract it. She closed her eyes and concentrated on locating the screwdriver. The pads of her fingers encountered cool metal and a hard edge. She followed the line of the toolbox up and tripped over the screwdriver sticking out. Holly grabbed it.

The van stopped and the engine died. Time was up. Holly's fingers trembled. She twisted so that she could wedge the screwdriver into the front pocket of her jeans. The handle stuck out, but her coat was long enough to cover it. If her kidnapper didn't look too closely, he would miss it.

The back door of the van opened, revealing a tall dark-haired man with a handlebar mustache. Holly recognized him immediately.

Eddie Daniels.

"Good, you're awake." Eddie sneered and grabbed her ankles with a hold tight enough to leave a bruise. He yanked and Holly yelped as she slid along the length of the van to the rear door. "Shut up. Do you know how much trouble you've caused me?"

Her trembles increased. Holly willed herself to remain calm. Eddie pulled her out of the van in front of a house. Debbie Daniels's house.

The cold air bit into Holly's cheeks and helped her shake off the remnants of cloudy thinking. He pulled a gun out of his pants. "Don't think about running. I'll just shoot you."

A metallic taste filled her mouth and Holly belatedly realized she'd bitten her tongue. Her muscles were rigid. She took a deep breath and forced them to relax, then nodded.

Eddie sneered. He turned to close the van doors. Holly reached under her coat and her hand wrapped around the handle of the screwdriver. The plastic bit into the soft flesh of her palm. "You attacked me outside the church."

He laughed. "Which time? You mean now or a few days ago?" Eddie got up in her face, close enough she could make out each pockmark embedded in his skin. "I'll help you out, Agatha Christie. It was both times."

She reared up with the screwdriver and jabbed him in the throat. Eddie howled, stumbling back.

A gunshot exploded. Holly expected to feel the bullet slam into her followed by gripping pain.

Instead, blood bloomed on Eddie's shirt and he dropped to the ground. Holly turned. A woman stood on the front porch in the shadows. She stepped into the light.

Holly gasped. "K-K-Kasey?"

"Do exactly as I say." Kasey raised the gun in her hands and pointed it at Holly. "Or the next bullet is for you."

She instinctively took a step backward. "What are you doing?"

"Don't think of running, Holly. Debbie and Gary are inside the house. If you give me trouble, I'll cause them pain."

Holly froze. Her gaze darted to the house before focusing back on her friend. Was she telling the truth?

Kasey's expression was hard, but she'd spoken with confidence.

Holly's stomach sank. There was no way she'd ignore Kasey's orders if it meant others would be harmed. Which is exactly what Kasey was counting on.

"Good, now that we understand each other, things will be much easier." Kasey waved the gun. "Drop the screwdriver on the grass. Then climb onto the porch and get in the house."

Holly did as directed. The interior of the house was well lit. Debbie was tied to a chair. The older woman's hair was a mess and a bruise bloomed on her cheek. Duct tape sealed her mouth. There was no sign of Gary.

Holly rushed to Debbie's side. "You hurt her. What are you doing, Kasey? What's going on?"

"Sit on the chair next to Debbie."

Holly hesitated, and Kasey pointed the gun at the older woman. "I will shoot her."

Mrs. Daniels said something behind the tape, but Holly couldn't make it out. The older woman glared at Kasey.

Holly couldn't risk it. Even if she could disarm Kasey, there was no guarantee Debbie wouldn't be hurt or killed in the process.

Please Lord. Please let Aiden figure out where we are.

Holly took a step and sat down in the chair. She expanded her chest and lifted her arms away from her body slightly. Hopefully, it would provide enough wriggle room to get free of the rope if a chance to escape arrived. "I don't get it, Kasey. Are you working with Gary? Or Michael? What are you doing?"

"I'm getting my freedom. Did you think I was going to

spend the rest of my life in this Podunk town? I have dreams, Holly, but I need cash to make them happen." Kasey wrapped another length of rope around Holly's midsection. She smirked. "I can see you're confused. Let me clarify things for you. Four weeks ago, Debbie drew up a contract with her attorney. If there came a time she couldn't live in the house, then I would become the owner."

Holly stared at her friend in horror. "You've been the mastermind of the attacks against me the whole time?"

Kasey grinned. "Surprise."

Like a jigsaw puzzle snapping into place, everything about the case suddenly came into stark clarity. "You needed me out of the way. I was helping Mrs. Daniels to stay in the house. Without me, she would go to a nursing home and you would become owner of the property. Then you could sell it to Michael for a handsome price."

"Not only did I need you out of the way, I needed Gary gone too. He didn't know Debbie had left the house to me, and as her son, he has the legal ability to challenge my ownership."

"So, you concocted a plan to kill me and frame Gary for it?"

"With Eddie's help." She knotted the rope. "It was supposed to be simple. Eddie would kidnap you, bring you to the property, and kill you in the barn. Gary parks his truck there all the time. I wanted him to find the body. It would make Gary the prime suspect."

Holly shuddered to think how close Kasey and Eddie came to killing her that night. "How did you get Gary to leave the bar?"

"I texted Gary and said something was wrong with his

mother. He rushed home to check on her but she was fast asleep because I'd drugged her. Debbie never knew her precious son was even here. He returned to the bar. But it was enough time to create a hole in his alibi."

"Except things fell apart when I fought back."

Kasey glared at her. "Yes. I had to get creative afterwards. I needed Gary to disappear so I could frame him for the subsequent attacks on your life. Eddie messaged Gary and asked to meet him in a cabin he'd rented in the woods. He drugged him and kept him there."

"You took the rifle from Mrs. Daniels's gun safe. That's why you were frazzled the morning we met. You had to come here to get the rifle and deliver it to Eddie before meeting us at the coffee shop." Holly couldn't believe she'd fallen for Kasey's fake friendship. "Eddie's the one who shot at us. Except he missed."

"I was pretty angry about that. How hard could it be?"

"Then he tried to run us off the road. In Gary's truck, I'm sure. Otherwise his would show damage from the impact."

Kasey nodded and flashed another smile. "The police will find Gary's truck at Eddie's cabin. They'll figure out that's where the two were hiding."

Holly twisted against the ropes. "Where is Gary now?"

"Upstairs. Drugged and tied up to the bed. Eddie arrived with him a few hours ago."

"You used Eddie to do your dirty work. What did you tell him, Kasey? That he would get some of the money?"

"Of course. How else could I get him to turn on Gary? Eddie's in way over his head and about to lose his business."

Her expression darkened. "But Eddie became a liability. So did Debbie."

Holly glanced at the older woman. "What do you mean?"

"I was hoping to convince Debbie to give me what's in her bank account along with the property. Most people aren't aware, but Debbie is loaded. Her daddy was an oil tycoon."

That explained why Kasey didn't kill Debbie once the woman had given her the house. Holly shifted in the chair. "You don't need to do this, Kasey. Debbie was kind to you. Let her go."

"It's too late for that." Kasey sauntered over to the table. Steel wool was spread out underneath some kind of contraption holding a battery. "Did you know that you can create a spark by touching a nine-volt battery to steel wool? It's very simple and effective."

A fresh wave of panic washed over Holly. "You're going to burn the house down?"

She laughed. "No, I'm going to make it explode. These old houses are famous for natural gas leaks. Throw in a spark and all my problems will be solved. I'll get the property. Gary won't be alive to challenge it and neither will Eddie. All of Debbie's relatives are dead in one fell swoop." She glanced at Holly again. "Oops. Almost forgot."

Kasey crossed the room and undid the handcuffs securing Holly's wrists.

"The police won't believe it's an accident if your hands are cuffed together." She smiled. It was evil and cold. "There now. The ropes will burn up in the fire and no one will be any wiser."

"Kasey, Michael Fisher isn't who he says he is. He's a criminal. A con man. He may not even have the money to pay you."

Kasey froze. She studied Holly for a long moment. "You're lying."

"No, I'm not. Mrs. Daniels did a background check on him and found out he's not a property developer at all. He's a criminal."

Debbie yelled something, but the words were muffled by the tape over her mouth. Holly couldn't make sense of what the older woman said. Kasey must've understood though. Her face turned red and she looked on the verge of a temper tantrum, but then she took a deep breath. "Never mind. This property is valuable. I'll find someone else who wants to buy it."

No. Holly couldn't let this happen. She struggled against the rope. "You won't get away with it. The police are going to figure out someone else was involved now that you've shot Eddie."

Kasey lifted the gun. "You're right, they will. Gary. This is his gun. I've already set it up nicely with that conversation we had at the coffee shop, remember? I told Aiden Gary and Eddie could be working together. It won't take much for Aiden to conclude the same once he matches the bullet that killed Eddie to this gun."

She disappeared into the kitchen. Moments later, a hiss came from the stove. The stench of rotten eggs filled the air. Holly's stomach turned. Debbie moaned.

Kasey practically skipped back into the room. She was a monster.

Holly struggled against the ropes. They ripped at the

fabric of her coat but refused to loosen. Kasey touched something and the battery started moving, slowly dropping toward the steel wool. The device would give Kasey time to leave the house before it exploded.

"Bye, Holly." Kasey waved before blowing a kiss. "Thanks for making me rich, Debbie. I promise to enjoy it."

She strolled to the door and left. Gas continued to fill the house. Holly's head swam, from the knock to her head or the scent of the gas, she couldn't tell. She pulled at the ropes, but they held fast. The battery dropped a little more. Beside her, Debbie bent her head in prayer. Holly joined her.

The door burst open. A broad-shoulder form appeared like an answer to Holly's prayers. Aiden. She hadn't heard the approaching sirens. She didn't know why and she didn't care to know. All that mattered was Aiden was here. Holly's heart soared.

She jerked her chin toward the table and yelled. "The battery on the table will ignite the gas."

Aiden knocked the battery away from the steel wool before it could fall and crossed the room to her in five strides. A dozen officers appeared behind him. Someone cut her bonds. Holly wanted to leap into Aiden's arms and never let go, but she couldn't. They weren't out of danger yet.

"Aiden, Gary is upstairs, tied up."

He turned to one of his officers. "Get these ladies and yourselves out of this house. Any spark could cause an explosion."

Before she could say anything, rough hands grabbed her. Holly caught a glimpse of Aiden disappearing upstairs.

Within moments, she was outside on the lawn. Ambulances raced down the drive. Debbie shook off the officers' hands and grabbed Holly's waist. "He'll be okay. They both will."

Holly didn't share the older woman's confidence. She stared at the open front door, prayers flooding her heart.

She loved Aiden. She needed to tell him.

Please Lord, give me the chance to tell Aiden how much he means to me. I've been so scared. Terrified of becoming my parents, but I'm not. Aiden was right. I'm not like them at all.

The house exploded.

Holly screamed. A wave of heat rushed her. Several officers pulled Holly and Debbie to the ground. Debris fell around them, peppering the grass with bits and pieces. The bulb from a string of Christmas tree lights landed on Holly's hand. She stared at it, the pain in her heart crushing her. She was going to spend Christmas without Aiden. Without the love of her life. Tears coursed down her cheeks.

No. No. No.

Holly tossed off the helping hands of the officers and stood. Thick smoke leaked from the charred remnants of the house. It moved and whirled with the wind.

A shadow appeared. Lumpy and inhuman. Holly's heart skipped a beat. She took a step forward. Was it Aiden? Or were her eyes fooling her?

The shape took sharper form. Aiden appeared carrying Gary in a fireman's hold. The police chief's uniform was ripped and his face blackened.

But he was alive. Aiden was alive.

Paramedics rushed forward, taking Gary from Aiden. Holly raced across the grass and leapt into Aiden's arms.

She sobbed, uncontrollable tears that stole her ability to speak.

Aiden swept his arm under her legs and carried her clear of the smoke. "Don't cry, sweetheart. Everything's okay."

"I thought..." She reached up to cup his cheek with her hand. "I thought I'd lost you."

"I went out the side door before the explosion. It was the closest escape route."

He set her feet on the grass, but she clung to him. Holly met his gaze. "I love you, Aiden. I love you. And I don't want one more minute to go by without telling you."

He blinked and then a slow smile crept across his face. "You love me?"

"I love you. Deeply. Get engaged, be married, have babies kind of love."

Aiden kissed her, sweet and long. Holly felt his heart in the kiss. It mingled with his fears and all the emotions there weren't words for. She didn't need him to explain. Holly already knew. Everything she'd thought in those moments after the explosion, he'd experienced after her kidnapping. They'd come close to losing each other.

Aiden ended the kiss and rested his forehead against hers. "I love you, too, Holly."

EPILOGUE

One week later, Aiden tucked Holly's hand in the crook of his arm. It was Christmas Eve, and the lights strung on the shops sparkled. The air was crisp and the night sky clear.

Holly smiled. "What a great idea to take a stroll after church service. The town is so pretty." She peeked at him through thick lashes. "You're nervous, Aiden. You have something to tell me."

If only she knew... Aiden took a deep breath and shoved those thoughts aside. There was business to take care of first. He'd considered waiting to tell Holly, but news would be all over town within hours anyway. Better she heard it from him.

"Kasey confessed this afternoon and made a deal with the District Attorney. She's going to prison for a long time."

Holly bit her lip. She stopped on the sidewalk and looked down the road. A tear sparkled on her cheek. Aiden brushed it away. "I'm sorry, sweetheart. I didn't want to upset you."

"You didn't. I'm just...I'm sad, that's all. Kasey could've

had love and happiness, but she decided greed was the better route. It's not what I wanted for her."

"None of us did."

Aiden felt pity for Kasey, but she'd made her choices. There were consequences for them. She'd been arrested within hours of blowing up the Daniels' house. So had Michael Fisher. He'd been caught trying to exit the country at the Mexican border. Although he didn't have anything to do with the attacks on Holly, it turned out Mrs. Daniels's research had been accurate. He was a criminal. Currently, Michael—actually Harry—was sitting in jail awaiting trial for the fraudulent schemes he'd run throughout Texas.

The case was finished. But that didn't erase the hurt.

Aiden sighed. "Kasey was fortunate because Eddie survived being shot. If he'd died, the District Attorney wouldn't have given her a deal at all. As it stands now, once Kasey turns sixty, parole will be a possibility."

"And Eddie?"

"The same. Neither of them will bother us again." He brushed a hand over her hair. "You're safe."

"I'm grateful." She leaned in and hugged him. "For you. For Mrs. Daniels. Even for Gary. He turned things around in the end by arranging for his mom to stay with her sister. I think Mrs. Daniels is going to be very happy there."

"So do I." He wrapped an arm around her waist, steering her toward the square and the Christmas tree. "Why don't we forget about all of that for the time being? It's Christmas Eve, and I want to spend it sneaking kisses by that gorgeous tree."

She laughed. "I won't argue with that. We raised three

times as much money for the Cutler Fund as last year. Did you know that?"

"No." He smiled. "I'm glad. You're going to help so many people with that money."

The square was empty, as Aiden had requested from the mayor and townsfolk. Cutler might have a rumor mill, but there was a time or two a secret managed to stay hidden.

He stopped by the tree. The lights sparkled in the branches and played off the gorgeous curves of Holly's face. Aiden ran a hand over her hair. "I haven't told you this, but there was a moment during the festival that's embedded in my mind, and it'll be there forever."

She turned to face him. Concern pulled at her mouth. "Aiden..."

He placed a finger over her lips. "No, not that one."

Yes, the memory of her kidnapping was forever engraved in his heart. But Aiden didn't want to dwell on the tragic moments from the last few weeks. They'd moved through the darkness. Together. Now it was time to rejoice. It was time to be happy.

"After the tree was lit, your eyes met mine." Aiden trailed his finger over Holly's lips and across her cheek. He tucked a silky strand of hair behind her ear. "The lights made your hair glow and you were smiling. In that moment, I knew I loved you. I'm sorry it took me so long to realize it. My heart...my heart had been hurt and I was worried about making the same mistake again."

"You aren't the only one who was scared." She smiled. "But I can talk about my fears with you, Aiden, and you help me through them. I never had that before."

If Aiden had his way, she would never go without it

again. He kissed her, his heart skipping several beats. "I love you, Holly."

He got down on one knee, reached into the pocket of his coat, and pulled out a small box. Holly gasped.

Aiden sucked in a breath. His fingers trembled as he opened the box, revealing a diamond ring. "I want to celebrate this Christmas with you as my fiancée. You're my best friend, Holly, and the love of my life. Please say you'll marry me."

Tears spilled over her lashes and onto her cheeks. "Yes, yes. I'll marry you."

He rose and kissed her until they were both breathless. Then Aiden backed away so he could slide the ring on her finger.

Holly started crying again. "This is the best Christmas of my life."

"The first of many, sweetheart. I promise you that." He swiped at her cheeks. "This is where you belong. It's your home and everyone here adores you."

He waved a hand and the square filled with people. Holly's clients, her grandparents, and Aiden's family. Church members. Townsfolk. All of them rushed to congratulate the couple.

The church choir burst into carols. Everyone else joined in. The scent of pine from the large Christmas tree carried on the wind.

Holly leaned over. "How did you pull this off?"

"It was easy. The town can keep a secret when there's good news involved." He hugged her closer and bent to whisper in her ear. "I wanted to give you the Christmas you never had. One filled with love and happiness. Family. Community."

"Thank you, Aiden." She cupped his cheek with her hand. "We're going to have a lifetime of happiness. There may be bumps and bruises along the way, but as long as I have you by my side, we can get through them."

"Yes, we can. It's forever, Holly. You and me."

"Forever." She stretched up and kissed him. "You and me."

ABOUT THE AUTHOR

Lynn Shannon writes novels that combine intriguing mysteries with heartfelt romance. Raised in Texas, she believes pecans and Blue Bell ice cream are must-haves for every household. Lynn lives with her husband, two children, an extremely spoiled dog, and a couple of chirpy lovebirds. You can find her online at www.lynnshannon.com.

ALSO BY LYNN SHANNON

Texas Ranger Heroes Series

Ranger Protection

Ranger Redemption

Ranger Courage

Ranger Faith

Ranger Honor

Triumph Over Adversity Series

Calculated Risk

Critical Error

Necessary Peril

Would you like to know when my next book is released? Or when my novels go on sale? It's easy. Subscribe to my newsletter at www.lynnshannon.com and all of the info will come straight to your inbox!

Reviews help readers find books. Please consider leaving a review at your favorite place of purchase or anywhere you discover new books. Thank you.

Made in United States
Troutdale, OR
12/20/2023

16166335R00063